Look what
Dangerous Liaisons miniseries...

About *Possession*...

"This is a classic Tori Carrington tale. It has all the
wonderful elements of category romance with
handsome, interesting characters, a 'bad boy,' a
'good girl,' meddling parents, meddling brothers,
and emotional and familial baggage galore. The sex
is steamy and provocative, woven nicely into the
reader's understanding of the characters.... This
book will appeal to all fans of Tori Carrington,
and future books in the series, if as good as this
one, will be something to anticipate."
—*The Romance Readers Connection*

"The atmosphere is as thick as the
New Orleans heat."
—*Romantic Times BOOKclub*

"The Rogue and the FBI Agent. *Possession,* the
latest by Tori Carrington, is a gripping whodunit
that is interwoven with hot, scintillating love
scenes. Don't miss the latest sizzling romantic
thriller from the dynamic Tori Carrington!"
—*BN.com*

"Sexy sizzler. The Carringtons at their very best,
and a look back at the Big Easy, when it was easy."
—*The Best Reviews*

Dear Reader,

When we first decided to set our DANGEROUS LIAISONS miniseries in New Orleans, Hurricane Katrina wasn't even a light breeze in the Atlantic. Now, well, after having witnessed the wrath of the storm and its devastating effects on one of our favorite cities and her many denizens, our hearts are filled with sorrow... and hope. Oh, we have no doubt that The Crescent City will rise again like a Phoenix rising from the ashes. Our hope is that the journey toward that end will be quick and as painless as possible.

In *Obsession,* the second title of three in the series, sexy Josie Villefranche's French Quarter roots stretch deep into the shadowy past of the infamous area. But when handsome Drew Morrison, aka The Closer, is assigned to force her to sell the hotel and onetime brothel that has been in her family for generations, he has no idea what he's up against....

We hope Josie and Drew's story captures a mere fraction of what was—and will someday soon be again—sexy and unique about this wonderful city. We've all given to the American Red Cross. Now may we suggest we turn our attentions to Habitat for Humanity to help in the rebuilding efforts? Go to www.habitat.org for more info. And keep an eye out for the final book in the series, *Submission,* in May.

With warmest wishes,

Lori & Tony Karayianni
aka Tori Carrington
P.O. Box 12271
Toledo, Ohio 43612
toricarrington@aol.com
www.toricarrington.com

TORI CARRINGTON
Obsession

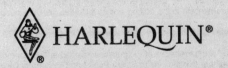

HARLEQUIN®

TORONTO • NEW YORK • LONDON
AMSTERDAM • PARIS • SYDNEY • HAMBURG
STOCKHOLM • ATHENS • TOKYO • MILAN • MADRID
PRAGUE • WARSAW • BUDAPEST • AUCKLAND

We dedicate this book to the
many victims of Hurricane Katrina.
Our hearts and thoughts are
with you now and throughout
the difficult struggles ahead…

ISBN 0-373-79247-6

OBSESSION

Copyright © 2006 by Lori and Tony Karayianni.

All rights reserved. Except for use in any review, the reproduction or utilization of this work in whole or in part in any form by any electronic, mechanical or other means, now known or hereafter invented, including xerography, photocopying and recording, or in any information storage or retrieval system, is forbidden without the written permission of the publisher, Harlequin Enterprises Limited, 225 Duncan Mill Road, Don Mills, Ontario, Canada M3B 3K9.

All characters in this book have no existence outside the imagination of the author and have no relation whatsoever to anyone bearing the same name or names. They are not even distantly inspired by any individual known or unknown to the author, and all incidents are pure invention.

This edition published by arrangement with Harlequin Books S.A.

® and TM are trademarks of the publisher. Trademarks indicated with ® are registered in the United States Patent and Trademark Office, the Canadian Trade Marks Office and in other countries.

www.eHarlequin.com

Printed in U.S.A.

1

THERE WERE TIMES when Josie Villefranche felt like the French Quarter hotel she owned and ran was still a brothel of legend.

Maybe it had something to do with the timelessness of her surroundings. Could be her mixed-race heritage was to blame. She was one quarter African American, like many of the women who would have run or worked in the onetime bordello over the past 150 years. Or perhaps her assistant manager was right in that one of her ancestors' ghosts still haunted the place, an ancestor who was rumored to have been one of the most successful madams in the Quarter's history.

Whatever the reason, this hazy Sunday afternoon was one of those times. She sat behind the check-in counter fanning herself with a starched lace fan. She'd found it among her *granme's* things in the fourth-floor room Josie had left untouched since Josephine Villefranche's death nearly a year ago.

Josie fingered the tattered edge of the fan, wondering where her namesake had picked it up. Was it a gift from a male admirer? Had she bought it herself at a local shop? And had she once sat right where Josie was sitting now, fanning herself, longing for someone, anyone, to walk through those front doors? Or thankful that all was quiet so she could catch a few moments to herself?

She released a long sigh. Of course, in the here and now, those quiet few moments were adding up, which was the reason Josie's mind now traveled to times long ago. The hotel had been doing very little business since the murder of that girl in 2D two weeks ago.

She glanced idly toward the winding, wooden staircase leading to the room in question. A sense of unease wound through her veins. Yesterday she'd been forced to cut her only maid, Monique, back to part-time. A temporary measure, she'd called it, until she could generate some business that would give the young woman more rooms to clean and more resources with which Josie could pay her. So as owner and operator, she, herself, had taken over some of the cleaning duties.

Merely being in room 2D earlier this morning had made her feel out of sorts. As if somehow the dead woman's soul remained behind, reluctant to leave until her killer was brought to justice, although all physical traces of her had long since been washed away.

Claire Laraway, that had been her name. Her one-night lover, and a onetime frequent customer of Hotel Josephine, Claude Lafitte, had been accused of her murder and arrested, then ultimately released. But not until after he'd taken a female FBI agent hostage and had shot off a round at the check-in desk to ward off New Orleans police officers. The bullet was still embedded in the front of the counter, just another part of the history of the old building. A building in dire need of repairs and sweeping renovations Josie couldn't afford.

If she didn't find a way to drum up some business, and quick, the hotel would become the property of the U.S. government by way of her overdue tax bills.

Then, of course, there was the matter of the killer still out there somewhere, on the prowl. A killer Monique half feared would strike at the hotel again. A view apparently shared by Josie's regulars, if the current vacancy of the rooms was any indication.

Josie caught herself waving the fan too quickly, kicking up a breeze that did nothing to cool the moisture that coated her skin. On the shelf under the top counter lay the latest of several offers made by a large national hotel chain to buy the Josephine. Offers she routinely refused to consider. Offers that offended her. Not because of the generous amount offered, but because Hotel Josephine was her birthright and it wasn't for sale. What would she do if she didn't have the business to run?

For as long as she could remember, the hotel had been a part of her life. It was included in one of her earliest memories, when her mother used to bring her there for brunch every Sunday after church. They'd sat with her grandmother in the courtyard restaurant in their best clothes—even now she could remember the delicate white gloves and hat she'd worn—enjoying café au lait and toast with jam.

Later, when her mother had met what she'd called "the one," the man who would change her life, there'd been no room in the picture for a girl whose black heritage was apparent, while her mulatto mother had been blond and blue-eyed. So Josie had been dropped off in front of the hotel with a plain paper bag holding her meager belongings, left staring at a grandmother who had been just as surprised to see her as she'd been to be there.

Josie smiled faintly. Of course, *Granme* had made the best of the situation, as she always had.

And Josie couldn't imagine how her life would have turned out had her grandmother not raised her.

Some may have viewed the work she'd done around the hotel beginning at a young age as an abuse of the child labor laws. Josie had seen it as inclusion. She'd preferred being around the adults, dragging a mop along the floor or stripping the beds and washing towels, to being on the street playing with other children her age. It had made her feel as if she were an adult. Someone in charge of her own life. She realized now that much of that desire to be older than her years stemmed from her never having known her father and from abandonment by her mother, but back then she'd only known a desire to be in control, however illusory that control was.

And now? Now that she'd inherited Hotel Josephine and was one missed tax payment away from losing her?

Often in past days she'd wondered what her grandmother would have done. Surely, she, too, had experienced tough times, and she'd obviously managed to come through them okay.

Josie would find a way, as well.

Footsteps on the banquette outside the hotel. She looked up to find a tall, wide-shouldered man in a suit considering the exterior of the place, then glancing inside. One of the few buildings loyal to French influences in the Quarter after the fire of 1794, the structure boasted double doors, a marble-tiled lobby with high ceilings and ornate cornices that spoke of glamorous times past. Her *granme* had loved plants, and they stood in every corner, giving the illusion of coolness to compensate for the lack of air-conditioning and insufficient ceiling fans. Josie squinted at the would-be customer, noticing his weathered yet expensive brown leather suitcase and his hat. Somewhere in his early thirties, he was an attractive man. But it was more than his good looks that made him that way.

"He's got that zing, that *it*," *Granme* would have said. "You stay away from men like that, Josie. Not a one of them is worth the heartbreak they'll bring."

Despite her advice, men seemed to break Josie's heart on a regular basis. While the city and its atmosphere of casual sex and impermanence might be partially to blame, she'd only ever found herself in the role of lover, but never partner. Never had she been referred to as someone's girlfriend or enjoyed the title of fiancée. It hadn't helped that four out of the five men she'd had temporary relationships with had been guests at the hotel. But since so much of her life revolved around the hotel, it was understandable that the majority of the men she crossed paths with would be guests, people just passing through. And leaving her behind without a backward glance when it was time to check out.

The visitor looked at something in his other hand. Josie realized it was one of the flyers Philippe Murrell, her assistant manager, had talked her into making up a couple days ago to distribute at the airport. She hadn't expected anything to come of the endeavor. Yet here was someone obviously brought to her doorstep as a result of Philippe's idea.

She rose to her five-foot, three-inch height and pretended busyness, praying for the man to come in.

When he finally did, she had to suppress a breath of relief, even though it would take a lot more than this one handsome man to save her hotel.

DREW MORRISON HADN'T REALIZED how far he'd fallen until he stood outside the run-down Hotel Josephine convinced he had the wrong address.

"The Closer." That's how he'd once been almost reverently referred to. He was an independent contractor who'd brokered multimillion-dollar deals on behalf of clients who were running out of options to obtain what they were after. From the employee-run window manufacturer putting a dent into a neighboring corporation's profits, to the stubborn casino owner who wouldn't give under pressure from his competitor, Drew eased his way into people's lives, became their friend, their confidant, and ultimately convinced them that selling would not only alleviate their worries and make them independently wealthy, but that it was also the brave, almost honorable thing to do.

Nowhere was it mentioned that it was the only thing to do.

Now he was reduced to penny-ante jobs like this one. Jobs similar to the type he'd taken on ten years ago when he'd been a wet-behind-the-years business grad, compliments of three years in the military serving overseas and the G.I. bill.

He ignored the sweat running down the back of his starched shirt under his Hugo Boss jacket. He guessed that's what happened when your loyal wife took you to the cleaners and screwed your divorce attorney without your knowing, walking away with everything you'd spent years building—and, in the process, costing you two important deals because your mind wasn't where it was supposed to be.

Drew stepped into the lobby of Hotel Josephine and took off his hat. One thing he'd never been was a complainer. He accepted full responsibility for the position he was in. After all, he hadn't seen behind Carol's greedy, money-grabbing ways. Had deluded himself into thinking she'd loved him, when, he'd figured out much too late, her affection had been a job to her, a means to an end.

And Carol had been very good at her job.

"Bonjour," the young woman behind the check-in desk greeted him, apparently busy doing something.

"Good morning." He put his suitcase on the floor, then placed his hat on the counter. "Are there any rooms available?"

From what he could make out of the quietness of the place, it was more than likely every room was available.

He watched a slender, honey-skinned hand reach for the guest book and skim through it, although the lined page she turned to was obviously empty.

"Room 2C should be cleaned by now."

She looked up at him.

And Drew Morrison felt like he'd just taken a hard one to the chest.

He couldn't be sure what it was about the

woman. For sure, she was attractive. Beyond merely attractive, if truth be told. She had a lush body that her simple, understated slip dress merely served to emphasize. Her dark hair hung in soft ringlets to her sleek shoulders. But none of that made her any different from countless other women he ran into on the street.

It was her eyes, he realized. The color of rich whiskey when you reached the bottom of a crystal tumbler. Eyes of a Caribbean witch who looked too old to be in this young woman. Eyes that could see straight to the core of a man, talk him into giving up his heart, before she left him to rot like garbage at the curb.

For a minute Drew forgot why he was there. Dangerous, that. He cleared his throat and tugged at his tie. "I'm in town for a convention at the Marriott."

Her expression remained the same. "How long do you want the room?"

He looked around, then remembered the flyer he'd serendipitously picked up at the airport. Copied onto light purple paper, it looked like the original had been haphazardly drawn up with Magic Marker. And added a little extra credibility to the story he would weave.

"This coupon still good?"

She accepted the piece of paper from him. It

was for a one-week stay at a rate lower than anything he would find anywhere else. And a hell of a lot lower than it would be when the hotelier who'd contracted Drew got his hands on the place.

"Yes." She picked up a pen from its stand. "So you'll be staying a week, then?"

He nodded and pulled his wallet from inside his suit jacket, wondering if it was always so hot down here in October. Oh, he'd been to the Crescent City before. Mostly to wine and dine marks and get them laid so they'd be more relaxed and open to his suggestions. "Sign here and you'll have the time to do this every weekend if you want" —that kind of shtick. But he'd never noticed how heavy the air was until today. Until he stood before the bewitching receptionist in front of him.

"Yes," he answered her question. "I figured since I'm down here for the Innovation in Auto Parts convention, I might as well make a vacation of it."

He cringed the minute the words were out. The key to selling someone on an identity was to keep it simple. The less said the better. Yet he found himself laying it on a little too thick here.

Those eyes focused on him again. "Why aren't you staying at the convention hotel?"

Reason Number One why you never offered up more than necessary: unwanted questions.

Drew switched his attention to his wallet and smiled. "I wanted something a little more...private."

He figured she was used to people saying that, because she didn't question him further.

"The full amount is due up front," she said, taking his information then turning around for a key that hung on a hook near the mail slots.

Drew's gaze lingered on the way the silky material of her dress clung to her long back and rounded bottom. She moved in a way that could inspire a poet. Slow and fluid, there was something almost ballet-like in her movements. Something alluring and sexy and very provocative.

"How about half now, half on checkout?" he asked.

Her movements slowed even more as she turned back to face him. "If you want the deal on the flyer, it's all due up front."

He pretended to consider her words, then offered up a grin with the money. "A woman who means business."

She smiled back, although it didn't reach her watchful eyes as she accepted the money.

Drew put his wallet away then extended his hand across the counter. "Thank you...I'm sorry, I didn't get your name."

"Josie." She briefly took his hand and then turned around to put the money into some sort of lockbox. He noticed her feet were bare and that she wore a chain of tiny shells around her left ankle. "Josie Villefranche."

Drew was mildly surprised she was the owner. His target.

He picked up his hat from the counter. Maybe this one last crappy job before he moved on to bigger and better things might not be without its fringe benefits.

2

DREW LET HIMSELF into room 2C, put his suitcase on the wrought-iron bench at the foot of the matching double bed, then crossed to the open French doors. He stepped out onto the narrow balcony and gripped the ornate railing, Bourbon Street spilled out like a strand of black pearls before him. He'd never actually stayed in the Quarter before. He might entertain his clients there, but he'd always stayed at the better hotels on the fringes of the famed district.

There was something almost…decadent about being there now. Although it was Sunday afternoon, he made out the sounds of a jazz band warming up in a bar across the street, watched as a few teenage girls, apparently on vacation, shopped for beads in a place a couple doors up, the faint smell of decay and beer and Cajun spices filling his nose.

A homeless black man wearing a crocheted

African hat and holding a trumpet case walked by the hotel, raising his hand to wave inside, presumably at the alluring owner, Josie Villefranche.

The view Drew took in was worlds away from the cityscapes he usually saw outside his hotel-room window. For that matter, it was certainly worlds away from the trailer park he'd grown up in outside Kansas City. In KC, being poor meant to the bone, no romance in the situation as families and single parents tried to make the rent and put cheap food on the table. Here…well, here poor seemed to be worn as a badge of honor. It didn't appear to be something you were, but a state you just happened to be in. In the French Quarter, strippers mingled with CEOs of large corporations, while in KC, most of the strippers would be lucky to meet a guy who worked at the Midland factory.

The contrast interested him. How would he have ended up had he been raised in a place like this, rather than the only son of a diner waitress in Missouri? A woman who'd smoked and drunk too much and had never let him forget where he came from? Who'd ceaselessly told him that his father was a useless, good-for-nothing deadbeat who had probably died when Drew was three to get out of paying child support?

Then again, you could change the story's setting, but the characters would still be the same, so Kansas City or New Orleans, it likely wouldn't have made a difference.

He stepped back into the room and looked around. It wasn't bad. Not too big. Not too small. The high ceilings helped, even though the ceiling fan did little more than stir the heat. The carved woodwork and cornices were original if painted over and chipped. The walls needed a fresh coat of paint, and he made out what looked like a water stain in one corner, but overall the structure looked solid. He ran his finger along the top of the dresser. It was also clean. A double wrought-iron bed, two matching nightstands and lamps, and the bench were the totality of the furnishings, although the room was large enough to accommodate a desk and a couple of chairs. He moved toward the bathroom and switched on the light. The black-and-white mosaic tile that might date back at least a century needed re-caulking, and the claw-foot tub could use some attention. The cloudy mirror needed to be replaced and the sink held iron stains. He switched the light back off. The entire hotel would need a complete renovation before it could even be considered as part of the Royal Emperor Suites empire.

Then again, that wasn't part of his job, questioning his clients' motives. It was how to get them what they wanted. And this particular client wanted Hotel Josephine.

The black, rotary phone on the nightstand rang. Drew stared at it, then crossed to pick up the receiver, idly wondering when the last time was that he'd seen such an old phone.

"Hello?"

"Good afternoon, Mr. Morrison." He recognized Josie's sexily husky voice. "I just wanted to let you know that our hotel offers a full menu and room service should you be interested."

Drew sat down on the bed, listening as the bed-springs squeaked. "That's nice to know. I might just take you up on that."

"Room service, then?"

He shrugged out of his jacket, hung it on one of the iron posts of the footboard, then began rolling up his sleeves. "Do you offer service downstairs?"

"Yes. In the courtyard."

"Then that's where I'll take my meal." After all, there was no time like the present to begin convincing the lovely Miss Villefranche that her life would be much easier without the hotel…and along the way perhaps entice her into sharing his bed while he was there.

"I NEED YOU TO RUN to André's and get an order of *crevettes* and *filet de truite amandine*," Josie said to Philippe as she swept through the swinging door into the kitchen.

The cook-slash-waiter-slash-busboy-slash-assistant manager sighed and began to undo the ties of his apron. "Couldn't talk him into only the gumbo and a salad?"

She took a twenty out of the amount Morrison had given her for the week's stay and handed it to her only staff member on duty at the moment. At any other time it took five to ten people to run the establishment. "Unfortunately, no."

She'd hired Philippe three months ago when Samuel, the hotel's assistant manager for the past fifty years, had died suddenly from a heart attack. Philippe had been a godsend at a time when Josie had been ill equipped to handle the loss of two very important people in her life so close together.

"Who's going to eat all this gumbo?"

Josie didn't provide an answer because Philippe didn't need one. The two of them would be eating the large pot of the New Orleans staple, with Philippe taking some of it home with him to his mother, although he was thirty and should have long since moved out on his own.

"Fine." He began moving toward the door that

would take him through the back where their only guest wouldn't see him. "He is a looker, that one, isn't he?"

Josie frowned at him. "I hadn't noticed."

"Hadn't noticed, my narrow behind. He could charm the paint off the walls, that one could." He crossed his arms in an exaggerated way.

"I don't think he's your type."

"Of course, he's my type. He's male, isn't he?"

Josie smiled. "Yes, but I don't think he's gay."

Philippe sighed. "Pity. Why does it seem like all the good ones want women?"

Josie shook her head as the door slapped closed behind his retreating back. She readied a sparkling glass along with a pitcher of water, put a basket of day-old bread into the microwave to warm it and therefore make it seem fresher, then went back out into the courtyard to serve Mr. Morrison.

"Ah, thank you," he said as she filled his glass. "Tell me, is it always this hot down here?"

It was a question Josie was asked often by tourists. While most seemed irritated with the thick heat, Morrison seemed merely to be asking a question. "It will cool down some soon," she said, glad he hadn't commented on the emptiness of the eating area.

"It doesn't even get this hot in the summer where I'm from," he said.

Josie removed the other three sets of silverware and wineglasses from the table. "Where's that?"

"Kansas City."

She didn't say anything as she moved to a cabinet near the kitchen door and put down the extra place settings. She'd never been outside the city. Had never had any cause to go anywhere else. While she'd heard somewhere down the line that her mother had ended up in Chicago, the northern city on Lake Michigan couldn't have seemed farther away from Josie had it been across the ocean.

"Excuse me," Morrison said, looking to catch her attention.

Josie turned toward him.

"What's that music?"

She'd switched on the tape system after she'd called his room, and he'd said he'd be coming down for his meal. "Zydeco."

He repeated the word. "Thanks."

Josie went back into the kitchen and leaned against the prep table. Long minutes later she was still standing in the same spot, breathing deeply, her hand resting against her collarbone. As much as she tried to ignore it, she was attracted to Drew Morrison with an intensity that surprised her. His hair was the rich color of an antique copper pot, the short cut failing to disguise that the strands were thick and wavy. The kind of hair a woman could thrust her fingers into and hold on to as she braced herself for a violent orgasm. He'd come downstairs without his jacket, his crisp white shirt-sleeves rolled up, and she saw that his forearms were muscular, his wrists solid. She'd caught herself staring at his hands as he'd picked up his water glass, noticing that his fingers were long and nicely tapered. The type of hands that would feel good against her bare skin.

It had been a long time since she'd been this aware of her sexuality and the fundamental need for human touch. Since before her grandmother had died, to be certain. She'd been so busy trying to keep up the hotel, she hadn't had time to look closely at the guests, talk to them. The brief contact she'd had so far with her current guest had made her register the deep blue of his eyes, the way they creased at the corners when he listened to her, and the fullness of his mouth—a mouth that would undoubtedly know what to do with a woman who needed to be kissed.

Is that what it was? she wondered. Had it been so long since she'd indulged herself sexually that her body was responding to the first good-looking man who crossed her path?

No. It was more than that. The instant the stranger had crossed the threshold of Hotel Josephine, an undeniable awareness had traveled over her skin like a lover's touch. It wasn't just that she was in the market for any man. She was drawn to Drew Morrison.

Something sounded outside the screen door. A rattle of a garbage can, maybe. A rat? A cat? There'd been a black cat around the Josephine for as long as she could remember, but this last one had stuck around the longest. She and her *granme* had named her Jezebel. Probably it was the old cat looking for her evening meal.

"Jez?"

She moved toward the back of the kitchen and stared out into the narrow alleyway. There was the sound again. Josie pressed her hand against the wood of the screen door, the hinges giving a low squeak as she peeked out toward where the hotel cans were lined up against the back wall.

Jezebel would have shown herself by now if it had been her.

"Shoo!" she said loudly, kicking the bottom of the can closest to her.

Nothing. No scurrying of a rodent or a hungry feline.

She stepped completely outside, the door slapping shut behind her. Picking up a stick, she poked at the next garbage can, then made her way down to the one after that. She'd reached the fourth one when a shadow leaped out behind the last can, running in the opposite direction.

Josie put a hand to her chest, as if to contain her rapidly beating heart. Jesus.

Philippe appeared from the direction the man had run.

"Damn homeless," he muttered. He handed her the bag of food from André's, then looked at her closer. "Are you all right?"

Josie swallowed hard, then managed a nod. "Um, yes. He just startled me is all. I thought he was a cat."

"An awfully big cat. More like a *rat*." He righted the empty can the man had overturned in his hurry to make haste. "You'd think he'd have figured out that we don't have anything to pick from here."

Josie led the way back inside the kitchen, vaguely wondering if she'd ever again have anything left to pick from.

Philippe washed his hands at the sink while she rearranged the food on a hotel plate.

"Do you want me to take it out to him?" he asked with a suggestive grin.

Josie shook her head. "No. I'll take care of him."

As she placed a sprig of parsley next to the trout, she ignored the many ways she'd been fantasizing taking care of Drew Morrison.

3

LATELY, NIGHT WAS the worst time for Josie. It was when she most profoundly recognized the reality that there was nothing she could do to help what was going on with the hotel. When long, quiet hours stretched out before her devoid of hope.

It was when the ghosts came out to play.

The muted night amplified the panting sound of the ceiling fan turning lazily above her. She looked up from the papers spread before her on the front desk to gaze out onto Bourbon Street. The stream of tourists' faces was occasionally interrupted by familiar faces from the neighborhood, some laughing, others drawn in thoughtful conversation. Some faces that were a lot more familiar up until recently, because they'd frequented the Josephine with their paying guests towed behind them.

She heard the creak of the stairs.

To conserve energy, she'd turned the dimmer on

the lights down to low, the small banker's lamp on the desk illuminating the papers before her.

There was only one guest, so she didn't have to look up to know that Drew Morrison was coming downstairs, probably to add his face to the others flowing past her door.

Josie concentrated harder on her work.

"Evening," Drew said quietly, his voice closer than she was prepared for as she made a note in the margin of one of the ledgers.

She looked up. "Evening."

In the low light he looked like any one of a hundred attractive men capable of attracting any one of a hundred attractive women. Women who filled the bars and restaurants and Bourbon Street itself.

Why, then, was she wishing she were one of those potential females?

She absently rubbed the back of her damp neck, suddenly all too aware of how alone she was at the hotel. A fact that normally didn't bother her. After all, she had been alone in the Josephine since *Granme* had passed away.

She swallowed hard and forced her gaze away from Drew and back to the ledger. Tomorrow she'd ask Philippe if he'd mind staying over for a night or two until she shook the uneasiness she'd been feeling lately.

Footsteps. She glanced up to find Drew walking toward the open doors. Probably to go on the hunt for one of those hundred attractive women. Instead, she watched him stop in the doorway and lean against the jamb, his legs crossed at the ankles as he slid his right hand into his pants pocket. His back was to her, so she felt safe in watching him without his being any the wiser. He seemed to be considering the foot traffic on the street much as she had earlier. A part of, yet separate from, the crowd.

"It's quiet." He cleared his throat and added, "At least it's quieter than I would have expected."

Josie lifted her brows. "Yes." She fiddled with the curls pressing against her forehead then slowly closed the book in front of her, placing it under the desk. "Would you like some recommendations on where to go?"

He grinned at her over his shoulder. "No. I think I can find my way around."

She had little doubt that he could. A man of his caliber could probably find his way around anywhere. And have a warm and willing companion in his bed for as long as he chose.

"That is if I was interested in going out."

Josie would have been surprised to find herself walking toward the door had she taken half a moment to think about it. But the truth was, she was tired of thinking for the night. Tired of thinking about the hotel and her problems. Her mind clamored for a few minutes of peace. Of quiet conversation.

Drew moved slightly as she leaned against the opposite doorjamb and crossed her arms in front of herself. A couple strolled by, arm in arm. Newlyweds, maybe. Or perhaps in the beginning stages of love when there existed no flaws, only the need for the other's company.

The reflection made her overly aware of the man next to her. Of how tall he was. Of the subtle scent of starch and fresh cologne.

"First time in New Orleans?" she asked quietly.

She felt his gaze on her. "Yes."

She nodded, going silent again as a group of young men who stumbled by apparently weren't holding their first beer. They hooted at a group of women half a block up, too young to realize the loud attention would get them nowhere. Too old to be indulging in such juvenile behavior.

"You?"

Josie looked at Drew. She wasn't prepared for the intensity in his eyes.

"Are you from here or a transplant?"

She felt the man next to her so completely she

nearly couldn't draw a breath. "Fifth generation New Orleanian."

"Where was your family from before then?"

Josie had never been asked that question before. She supposed because her answer was usually all that the other person needed.

"Carrefour, Haiti."

"Ever been?"

She shook her head, keeping to herself that she'd never really traveled outside the city and its surrounding bayous.

She considered him for a long moment, trying to ignore the slow thud of her heart at being this close to him. "Anyone ever tell you that you ask a lot of questions?"

His grin was slow and wide. "All the time."

"Part of your job?"

There was an almost indistinguishable stiffening of his limbs although he hadn't moved. "You could say that."

It seemed that the man liked to ask questions, but he didn't like answering them.

Josie cleared her throat and turned her attention back to the street. Most men she crossed paths with were the same. It was almost as if they wanted to adopt a different persona while in the decadent city. Live out some kind of anonymous fantasy. Many of them forgot that she and the natives were just like everyone else. That they hadn't been placed there strictly for their amusement or as players in whatever fantasy they'd concocted on the plane ride down.

If it was disappointment she was feeling that Drew was just like every other man who visited the city, she told herself she was being stupid.

Josie Villefranche was a rare and unusual beauty.

And the faint line that marred her lovely brow told Drew he'd just said something to upset her.

The mellow almost longing sound of a saxophone drifted out of the open door of the club across the street, lending a certain moment-outside-of-time element to the atmosphere.

When he'd decided to come downstairs to try again to connect with the exotic hotel owner—both to further his business intentions and to combine a bit of business with pleasure—he would never have expected her to stand next to him, inviting conversation. During dinner earlier, she'd disappeared into the kitchen, sending out a dark-haired young man, who'd smiled at him too widely, to handle him for the rest of his meal.

Now…

Well, for a moment he'd been lulled into a false sense of normalcy. Into thinking for a dangerous moment that he was there for no other reason than to enjoy her company, instead of her company being a bonus on top of something more important.

He slid his hand from his pocket and gestured to the hotel. "You work here long?"

A faint smile that seemed inspired more by irony than by humor. "You could say that." She looked at him.

It didn't take a NASA scientist to know that she had just turned his words back on him.

Intriguing.

"Do you like it?"

That seemed to catch her off guard. As if perhaps she'd never really stopped to think about the enjoyment factor of her responsibilities. He, of course, knew she outright owned the place. He also knew she had a female cousin who was breathing down her neck trying to extort money from her. And that she had a tax bill that was accumulating more penalties and interest on a daily basis. Not to mention that she hadn't had a full paying guest before him since the murder that had taken place in the hotel a couple weeks ago.

Now what was there not to like about that?

She gave a small shrug that drew his gaze to the

golden, damp skin of her bare shoulders. "That's like asking me if I like my right arm. Or my toes." She turned her whiskey eyes on him. "It's so much a part of me that I don't much think about it beyond it's always been there."

Drew had to look away. Her words hit a chord with him he was loath to dwell on.

"So the place is yours, then." It was a statement more than a question.

She lightly bit on her plump bottom lip and nodded. "My *granme,* my grandmother, left it to me when she passed away last year. It's been in my family for generations."

Drew knew that. He also knew that her grandmother had been a shrewd old woman who'd also refused to sell. He wondered if shrewdness ran in the veins of the Villefranche women. And he referred to *women* because as far as he could uncover during his extensive investigation, there were no Villefranche men.

Drew pretended to look around. "Is it always this quiet?"

"No. It's been a bit less busy than usual lately." A couple walked by in front of them.

"Hey, Frederique," Josie greeted.

The overly made-up woman with a stretchy, low-necked top and short skirt smiled at her. "Hey, yourself, Josie girl." She looked between them to the hotel lobby beyond. "How's business after, well—" her gaze flicked to Drew's face "—you know?"

Josie smiled. "Fine. It's fine. Back to normal for all intents and purposes."

"They catch...the person?"

Josie said they hadn't.

The Quarter Killer. That's what the murderer of the woman two weeks ago had been called by the local paper, the *Times-Picayune*. Drew hadn't thought much of it. He'd reviewed the info he could get his hands on and suspected that the police had arrested the right man to begin with, and that Claude Lafitte had been released only because his older brother had married the daughter of a rich New Orleans businessman.

The woman stopped, nearly causing her overweight male companion to run into her back. "I think we'll stop here," she said.

The man pushed up his glasses, a nearby streetlight glinting off his balding head. "I thought we were going to your place?"

The prostitute Josie had called Frederique smiled and smoothed back the tufts of hair over each of his protruding ears, giving him a loud kiss. "I can't wait that long, baby. I want you now."

She kissed him again, then edged him between Josie and Drew into the lobby.

"My regular room," she whispered. "Oh, and he's got money, so don't worry about overcharging, if you get my drift."

Josie's gaze met Drew's and he wondered if she would raise the room rate for the drunken john.

"A regular?"

"You could say that."

Then he watched as Josie left him to go check in her latest guests, and just like that Drew lost his tentative connection with her.

"Mr. Morrison?"

He jerked to look at Josie, who had stopped halfway to the desk. He was so taken off guard that he didn't think to tell her to call him Drew.

"Would you like a nice, ice-cold glass of tea?"

Drew smiled. "Yes. Yes, I'd like that."

4

ONLY DREW HADN'T GUESSED he'd be drinking that tea alone.

He lay back in his double bed staring at the whirling fan and the shadows playing across the ceiling. It was somewhere around 3:00 a.m., and in the room next to his the squeak of bedsprings had finally stopped along with the moaning he suspected was faked, but he couldn't be sure.

What he *was* sure about was that the sound of a couple having sex, albeit it professional sex, ratcheted up his own growing desire for the elusive hotel owner.

He rubbed his forearm draped over his brow then sighed. It was hot. Hotter than he could remember it being for a long time. Or perhaps his keen awareness of it was due to the lack of air-conditioning.

His gaze fixed again on the ceiling. But not to look at the shadows there. Instead, he tried to detect any more sounds from the room two floors above his. A room he assumed was Josie's because when he'd been standing on the balcony over the hotel entrance, he had heard her lock up and shortly thereafter had followed the sound of her footfalls up the stairs. There had been no more customers. But earlier, at around midnight when he'd been sipping his tea—alone—in the open doorway, he'd watched as a walking tour of some sort had stopped in front of him and a guy in period clothing had outlined the happenings of a couple weeks ago. The nine or so tourists had stared at him and the hotel in awe. Then the guide had gone into a story that went back much farther than recent history, and had made the murder of Claire Laraway pale by comparison.

"It's said that Hotel Josephine is still haunted by the ghost of the original owner, Josephine Villefranche, who wanders the halls at night. Some say she seeks revenge for the wrongs done to her. Others say it's a heart-wrenching attempt to find her lost love—the man who took her life during the fires of 1794."

Drew had saluted the group with his empty glass, then headed upstairs to his own room.

He wondered how Josie felt about being associated with such notoriety.

From somewhere in the hotel he heard a phone

ring. He suspected it was the main phone. He looked up at the ceiling again, wondering how long it had been since Josie Villefranche had gotten a break from all the hotel's demands.

And wondering how he might convince her that was exactly what she wanted most in the world.

JOSIE'S HAND STOPPED its rhythmic motion of smoothing lotion over her calf as she stared at the ringing telephone. While the city might never sleep, calls after eleven were rare. And given her recent experience with late-night calls, she wasn't sure she wanted to answer this one.

Still, she had three guests to consider. And, true to form, this late-night caller had no intention of giving up until she answered.

On the eighth ring she slowly picked up the receiver.

"Hello?"

No response.

She breathed a sigh of relief. They'd hung up.

She was about to return the receiver to its cradle when a low, familiar voice asked, "Josie Villefranche?"

Familiar not because she knew the owner of it. But because she'd heard it often in the past few months.

"I know you're there, Josie."

The caller was a man. That was all she knew. Well, that and the fact that his sole intent was to frighten her.

"I hear the murdered girl's ghost is still in room 2D, Josie."

Since the calls had begun long before Claire Laraway's murder, she had never linked the two.

Until now...

"She wants some company."

"Who is this?"

But she knew her whispered inquiry would go unanswered.

Instead she heard an eerie chuckle. "Good night, Josie. Sleep well."

Then the line went dead.

Josie slowly hung up the receiver, her blood flowing thickly through her veins. She rose from the wrought-iron chair her grandmother had given her as part of a vanity set when she was fourteen and moved toward the open French doors, looking into the dark night beyond the lights of Bourbon Street.

When she'd received the first call some months ago, she'd assumed it might be someone who had once stayed at the hotel who was playing an awful prank. But when the calls continued, with no pattern that she could make out, a deep sense of dread and fear had pierced her initial nonchalance, leaving her creeped out for a long while afterward.

Could the caller be Claire Laraway's killer? Is that what all this had been leading up to? Was there some sicko out there who had targeted her for some sort of demented plan and was even now playing it out?

A sound caught her attention. She jumped then looked down to find that Drew Morrison had stepped out onto his balcony two floors below, his slacks hanging low on his hips, his well-defined torso bare. Had the ringing phone awakened him? Or was he, like her, incapable of sleep just now?

She didn't realize that he'd looked up and spotted her until he said something.

"Is everything all right?"

Josie grew aware of her faraway thoughts and the expression she might be wearing as a result of her disturbing midnight caller.

"Yes…I'm fine." She crossed her arms to ward off a shiver. "Is there anything else you need?"

She caught the way he scanned her body. She wore a light slip that clung to her damp skin and left very little to the imagination. The intensity of his gaze made her nipples tighten beneath the silky material.

If there was one thing she'd learned very young, it was how to read a man's expression. And the expression Drew wore told her that he did, indeed, want something, if not need it. And that something was her.

The fact that she wanted him right back didn't help cool her body temperature.

She cleared her throat. "Very well then. Good night, Mr. Morrison."

She stepped back inside her room and closed the screen door.

She had little doubt that his quiet, sexy chuckle would resonate in her mind, and her dreams, well into the night.

LATE THE FOLLOWING MORNING, Josie accepted the package of cleaned and pressed guest linens and towels from the service. She stared down at the bill that had been payable on delivery. If things didn't change soon, she'd have to see to the washing herself.

"Did you get the supplies?"

She blinked up at Philippe who'd appeared beside her behind the desk.

Supplies…

She handed him the plain brown wrapped linens. "No. Why don't you see to it right after you take these up to Monique? She should still be on the second floor."

He didn't look pleased. But Philippe's displeasure at the moment was the least of her concerns. If she didn't come up with a plan to turn things around and quick, they'd all be very displeased indeed. Monique and Philippe would be without jobs…and Josie would be without her hotel.

After only a couple hours sleep, she'd gotten up early and had come down to brainstorm ideas to get the Josephine back on track. Aside from a list of names she'd taken from the phone book of attorneys she hoped might help her with her tax problem, she'd made up a page of Rent One Night, Get One Night Free coupons, which she would have Philippe copy for her and then she would give out to her onetime regulars like Frederique.

"Josie? Is everything okay?"

She looked up to find Philippe still standing next to her with the linens in his hands.

"You don't look so hot, *chérie*."

She straightened the papers in front of her. "Have I ever told you that you have a way with the ladies, Philippe?"

He grinned at her. "No. But then again that's not exactly on my list of priorities either."

She gave him an eye roll and laughed, although with half the heart she might have.

"Has something happened?" he asked.

She shrugged. "I got another one of those calls last night is all."

Of course, that wasn't all that was bothering her, but it would fill the bill for now. The rest…well, the rest she couldn't unburden on Philippe.

He put the package back down on the desk. "I've been telling you forever that you need to get your phone system updated. You're still using rotary technology when caller ID might be able to nip the little problem of your midnight caller in the bud."

"You told me callers could block that."

She thought again about alerting Homicide Detective Chevalier about the calls. If there was even a remote possibility that the caller could be connected to the murder…

She gestured Philippe away. "Anyway, with business the way it is, we'll be lucky to have phones at all by next month."

Philippe still hadn't moved.

She raised her brows. "It might be a good idea for you to at least look busy in case, you know, I decide I can cut your pay or eliminate your job altogether."

He squared his shoulders and looked a gesture away from saluting her. "Yes, sir. I mean, ma'am."

He picked up the package then took the stairs two at a time. Josie shook her head and turned to collect the lockbox so she could give him the money for the kitchen supplies he needed.

"I think that's the first time I've seen you smile."

Drew.

Josie recognized the smooth timbre of his voice without looking. Of course, that might also have to do with the fact that he was her only current paying customer. But the way tiny bumps raced along her skin wasn't how she usually reacted to regular customers.

"Mr. Morrison." She turned toward the desk.

He was wearing a badge that had the Marriott motif on it along with the name of an auto-parts organization and his own name. He followed her gaze.

"Oh. I forgot I still had this on." He put down his briefcase and pulled the elastic fastener over his head, tousling his hair.

"Uh-oh. The smile's gone."

Josie couldn't help giving him another. He looked like a breath of fresh air in a stiflingly hot room. He was as welcome as he was unexpected.

"Conference let out for the day?" she asked, counting out the money then returning the lockbox to its spot behind her.

"No. Just decided Gasket Technology of the Future wasn't going to do it for me this afternoon. So I decided to play hooky."

Hooky. How youthful the word sounded. And how carefree. Had she ever played hooky from anything? School? Work? She couldn't remember a time when she'd ever shrugged off her responsibilities and given herself over to spontaneity.

She couldn't remember a time when she'd ever wanted to.

But somehow standing there looking into Drew's face…well, she wished she could escape from the worries of her life for a few precious hours. After all, it wasn't like the worries would go anywhere. They'd still be there when she got back.

Philippe came down the stairs.

Josie looked at Drew. "So did you have anything planned to fill your day?"

He looked mildly surprised by her question. "Actually, I was going to try to tempt you into becoming my private tour guide for the afternoon, but I didn't think I stood a snowball's chance in hell."

Josie edged out from behind the counter. "Philippe, mind the store for a couple hours. It looks like snow to me."

DREW COULDN'T BELIEVE his streak of good luck. Not only had Josie agreed to stroll through Jackson Square and then down Bourbon Street with him, she actually appeared relaxed and, yes, happy.

Why she'd decided to come out with him, he couldn't be sure. But he wasn't about to tempt fate by questioning whatever plan the gods had in mind.

"So you grew up at the hotel," he said quietly, watching the play of dappled sunlight on her tight, black curls.

She nodded then watched her feet as they walked. She wore flat sandals with straps that wrapped around her ankles, the ring of shells around her left ankle clinking as she moved. "In essence, yes." She squinted at him. "And you? I mean, I know you were born in Kansas City, but you haven't really said anything beyond that."

Despite the heat of the day, Drew slid his hands into his slacks pockets, to hide the fact that he'd clenched them. "Nothing much to tell, really. My father left my mother before I was born. Although I think you actually have to be a couple before one can leave the other." He chuckled without humor.

"So you think your mom lied to you?"

He stared at her. "Yes. Yes, I do. I think she'd had a one-night stand, or a brief relationship with someone, someone who never had a clue she was pregnant. Then she blamed everything on him."

"Sounds familiar."

Drew was curious. "Oh?"

Josie smiled softly. "Yes. The identity of my father is as sketchy as yours, and my mother always cursed him, although they'd never been married. *Granme* used to say something about my mother having dated one man too many." She shook her head. "I never understood exactly what she meant until I got older."

Drew was surprised by the lack of bitterness with which she shared her past.

"Do you and your mom get along now?" she asked him.

"No. She died five years ago."

"Oh. I'm sorry."

He lightly grasped her arm to prevent her from running into a street mime painted in silver and dressed to look like a statue.

She said, "My mother's still alive. Living somewhere in Chicago, I think. She hasn't been in contact with the family for over fifteen years. I couldn't even find her to tell her *Granme* had passed."

"You seem okay with that."

Josie shrugged, her eyes clear and lovely. "I am, I guess. I mean, my *granme* never excused her actions when she left her old family behind to start a new family, but she never cursed her either. Merely said that everyone had their path to walk, and that was hers."

"While yours was with your grandmother at Hotel Josephine."

She smiled at him, challenging the sun for brightness. "Yes."

Josie had turned them down a side street and he followed, noticing the quietness of the road compared to the constant busyness of Bourbon. The clap of her sandals sounded against the pavement.

"And the hotel…" She drifted off, staring at some undefined point in front of them. "The hotel is almost like family to me. I've lived in it for so long, become acquainted with her ghosts, polished her banisters, mopped her floors so many times that—"

She stopped not because she'd run out of words. But rather because she'd looked at Drew and seen in his eyes the sudden urge to kiss her.

And before he knew it, he was doing just that.

He wasn't sure what had inspired the move. It could have been the way she spoke with such love and longing, her pink, bowed lips moving, her eyes as warm as melted brown sugar. Whatever the reason, his kiss had little to do with his ulterior motives and everything to do with the woman who blinked at him in surprise and wonder.

Then she easily returned his kiss.

5

JOSIE'S BREATH LEFT HER at the first touch of Drew's mouth against hers. One moment she'd been walking, talking about…she couldn't remember. The next, he was gently turning her toward him, brushing his fingertips against her jaw, and kissing her as if he hadn't been able to help himself.

And the surprise she read in his eyes surely had to be reflected in her own.

When Drew Morrison had walked through the doors of the Josephine yesterday, the last thing on her agenda had been personal involvement of any sort. She'd traveled down that road before and knew the dead end she would eventually crash into.

But what she hadn't factored into the equation was that she'd gone into her previous luckless relationships without using her head. Each interlude had offered an opportunity just to feel.

And feeling was exactly what she was doing

now, as she stood in the middle of the street kissing an almost perfect stranger.

And enjoying it more than was safe.

Drew's tongue slid along her bottom lip, then dipped inside her mouth. He tasted like coffee and powdered sugar from the beignets they'd gotten at Café Du Monde. He tasted like one hundred percent man. Like desire and want and need all rolled up into one nicely wrapped package.

And Josie wanted more than anything to open it.

She splayed her fingers against the hard wall of his chest and broke the kiss.

"That was…" She drew a ragged breath, her eyes turned downward. "Unexpected."

Drew chuckled, the sound rumbling against her palm. "Is that a good thing or a bad thing?"

Josie stared at her short, unpainted nails against his expensive Egyptian broadcloth shirt. She was dark to his light. Poor to his wealth. Yet on a primal level they emerged equals.

She knew instinctively this man could make her body feel things as it never had before. But it was time to bring her head into the equation for a change.

"Look, Drew," she said, meeting his gaze, "I don't want either one of us to go into this with our eyes closed."

"Into what?"

She smiled softly. "I'm not naive. Most of the men who come down here are looking for a brief, no-strings-attached affair with a native."

"Josie—"

"No, don't interrupt." She twisted her lips. "I'm not passing judgment on you, merely stating fact. And the fact is there is no hope for a future beyond this moment. I understand that."

He ran the back of his index finger across her brow. "Josie, we just kissed."

"No lies, Drew," she said quietly. "That's all that I ask. No lies. What develops—if anything develops between us—is temporary. I don't want either one of us to pretend otherwise. That's all. That's my only request."

He stared at her for long moments then nodded. "Okay."

A simple word, really. But one that immediately smoothed the tension from her shoulders. Wiped the memories of the other times when men she'd been involved with had sworn never to lie to her then proceeded to do exactly that.

She kissed him again, long and hard. "I, um, think we'd better get back to the hotel."

"Best idea I've heard all day."

She laughed softly. "I need to relieve Philippe so he can do his job instead of mine."

She began walking. She felt Drew's hand on her elbow then shivered as he moved it down to grip her fingers in his.

"Would I be moving too fast if I asked for the pleasure of your company for dinner tonight?"

Pleasure. Yes, it would definitely be a pleasure to dine with Drew.

"No. You wouldn't be moving fast enough. How about a late lunch? Say at around three?"

DREW FELT AS IF HE'D NEVER be able to get rid of the light sheen of sweat that covered his skin. Of course, he acknowledged that the thick heat wasn't entirely to blame, even though it definitely was getting to him, since he'd been careful to bring only the clothing a businessman attending a professional convention would need. Suits to reflect a first timer's unfamiliarity with the Crescent City.

But the clothes and weather weren't the only reason for his discomfort. Rather his anticipation of promised time alone with Josie Villefranche had him in a constant heated state.

It had been some time since he'd been with a woman, and he was afraid his body was showing him exactly how long. After his ex had pulled the stunt she had on him, he'd been subconsciously leery of becoming involved with anyone, even physically. The laser-like focus he'd put on re-building his career also explained the ease with which he'd steered clear of women.

But Josie…

While he tried telling himself his interest in her was merely professional and physical, there existed in the pit of his stomach the sensation that there was something more to his attraction to the mysterious hotel owner. He'd listened as she'd shared her story about her mother and grand-mother, told of her attachment to the hotel, and he'd felt admiration for her fighting spirit and loyalty to the establishment.

And guilt that it was his job to take it away from her any way he could.

He stood outside a small shop nearer the more touristy area of Bourbon Street, not really seeing the T-shirts or the colorful beads. If he knew what was good for him, he would forgo his three o'clock date to meet Josie back at the hotel. Offer up a story about a superior requesting his presence at the convention. He'd told her he'd hoped she didn't think he was going too fast. In reality, he was beginning to think he was. A concept that had never occurred to him before. He'd always been painfully careful about personal attachments, in-cluding with his ex-wife. But no matter how cautious he'd been, he'd still gotten burned by a woman who'd turned out to be far too similar to his mother.

And while Josie couldn't have been further away from Carol in looks, temperament and background, and she was obviously fiercely independent, she was in financial trouble. And he'd learned long ago that money, or rather the lack of it, made people do unexpected and hurtful things. It was that very fact that he exploited in his job every day.

Then why was his gut twisting into knots at the prospect of enjoying Josie's company at the same time he talked her into selling the hotel?

Conscience.

He'd once been accused of not having one. It had been early on in his career and he'd befriended an older man, Bernard Glass, who had built up his shoe factory over a period of fifty years into a moderately viable business he'd hoped to leave to his grandson, who would be graduating college in a year. Then one very successful television show had written the lead character as a Glass shoe fanatic and overnight the old man's orders had quadrupled.

And his factory had become prime pickings for an Italian clothes designer who had had his eye on adding a shoe company to his impressive list of businesses.

"Can I help you find something, sir?" a voice interrupted his thoughts.

Drew stared at the young saleswoman.

He found himself fingering a necklace of tiny shells like the ones Josie wore around her slender ankle. He removed his hand. "No. No, thank you."

He strolled down the street in the opposite direction of the hotel, not due to meet Josie there for another fifteen minutes, his mind still on Glass and his company.

Back then, Drew had still been testing the boundaries of how far he would go to close a deal. He'd had the grandson investigated and discovered David had more than a taste for gambling. Worse, he was in trouble way up to his neck, owing a loan shark near Boston University, which he attended, far more than he could ever hope to repay on his own.

Drew had shamelessly used the information, and played up the grandson's lack of direction in life beyond finishing university, to convince the old man he needed to sell his company rather than leave it to the grandson.

A month later Drew had received a visit from the old man, who had finally figured everything out.

"You have no conscience, Drew Morrison. And one day you'll be paid back several times over for all the wrong that you do."

He'd tried to deny his part in the scheme. Strangely, he'd grown attached to the old man, who had built his company with his own two hands. But Bernie wouldn't hear him. He'd merely said his piece and left Drew with a new awareness of boundaries he hadn't recognized before.

From there on in he'd left families out of the business equation, no matter how easy the target. He'd relied solely on his own skills to accomplish the task he was being paid for—most times very well.

Then there was Josie…

Certainly, he'd come across his share of marks attached in some strong way to their companies or interests. But usually they were neglecting another part of their lives that was easily amplified. Children who wanted more of their attention. A hobby that could be turned into a career. Sometimes he even allowed himself to believe he was doing the marks a favor by helping them improve their lives, although that feeling never lasted more than a couple of seconds if only because he knew his clients were the ones benefiting monetarily. After all, a mark wouldn't be a mark if that person didn't have something the client wanted.

In Josie Villefranche's case, he'd never expected he'd be the one doing the wanting and that what he wanted had absolutely nothing in common with what his client wanted.

JOSIE SWIPED THE BACK of her wrist across her forehead as she stirred the boil pot on the old, industrial stove in the kitchen of the Josephine. She'd coerced Philippe into looking after the front desk again, telling him she wanted to take care of dinner tonight. He hadn't said anything. After all, they often traded spots if just to keep things interesting, or if she felt the itch to keep her cooking skills fresh.

But she had received a raised brow when she'd instructed him to send Drew back to the kitchen when he arrived.

That was *if* he did arrive. She looked at her watch. It was ten past three. Considering their kiss on the street that morning, she'd half expected him to stick around the hotel until the time she'd set for their late lunch.

Instead, he'd left and had yet to return.

Second thoughts, maybe?

She shut off the fire under the pot then moved it from the burner, continuing to stir.

Since their spontaneous connection, she'd been running their kiss and their conversation through her mind, over and over again. She'd made the request of their temporary liaison for her own emotional safety. But by doing so had she taken the thrill out of it for Drew? Having a woman fall head over heels for you then leaving her when it was time to go might be part of the fantasy. By stating up front that she had no intention of falling for him, had she ended their liaison before it had a chance to get interesting?

Josie realized she'd stopped stirring and continued, doubling her efforts. Even if Drew wasn't around for the meal, she and Philippe would enjoy eating something other than the staple gumbo they kept on hand for potential guests.

The old black cat that called the hotel home jumped up onto the counter next to the burner.

"Jezebel, what are you doing in here?" She plucked up the curious feline before she could do any damage and carried her to the back door, where she put her outside. Careful to prevent the cat from getting back in, she filled the bowl next to the door with dry food. For some reason she couldn't put her finger on, being there made her uneasy.

The inner hotel telephone extension on the wall rang, startling her.

She backtracked to the stove, wiped her hands on her apron and answered it.

"He's on his way to the kitchen."

Josie's heart nearly beat straight out of her chest.

She thanked Philippe, then hurried back to the pot, trying to regain control over herself.

It was just a meal, for crying out loud. No reason to be so nervous.

She supposed it might be because she had half expected him not to show and had gotten used to the idea. That must be the reason for the butterflies in her stomach. But when she turned her head at the sound of the door swinging open and saw Drew, she knew she was dead wrong.

It was the fact that her attraction for him seemed to have doubled since earlier that had her heart pounding in her chest.

And if the dark awareness in his eyes was anything to go by, his desire for her was just as strong.

She smiled, trying to force a swallow down her tight throat. "Come on in. I hope you don't mind, but I thought we'd eat in here."

He blinked as if just breaking from some sort of trance, then looked at the chopping block in the middle of the room she had set with checkered place mats, linen-wrapped silverware and a dozen candles in different colors and sizes. A bottle of red wine was breathing next to two sparkling crystal glasses.

She'd done so much rattling on during their walk earlier that she was armed with a thousand and one questions she wanted to ask him. Questions that vanished now. She could barely focus enough to keep from ruining the simple yet very Creole meal she'd prepared.

Drew hadn't moved from the doorway.

She stopped stirring and picked up two bowls from the sideboard. After filling them, she switched on the flame beneath the boil pot, then carried the bowls to the cutting board.

"Pour the wine?" she suggested.

Finally, he moved from the doorway, slowly doing as she asked. After she finished cutting the thick, crusty bread she'd placed on the board earlier, he handed her a glass. She looked to find his eyes regarding her soberly.

"To the strangers we meet along the way," she said quietly.

He clinked his glass lightly against hers and drank.

She broke eye contact then climbed up on one of the two stools. "This is best eaten hot."

He sat across from her. "What is it?"

"Yam and crabmeat bisque. Have you ever had it?"

"Can't say as I have."

She took a piece of bread. "It's best eaten this way." She scooped a bit of the thick soup with the bread then reached to put it in front of his mouth. He cracked his lips and accepted the soup-drenched morsel. He chewed silently.

"Do you like it?"

"My compliments to the chef."

Josie looked away quickly. The recipe was one her *granme* had shared with her, teaching her how to make it when she was eight and was no longer a danger around an open flame. Over the years, she'd learned to experiment with the spices herself and even her *granme* had proclaimed hers the best she'd ever tasted.

"Most Creole food is meant to be eaten with your fingers," she said. "I hope you don't mind."

His gaze seemed to linger on her hands as she licked bread crumbs from the pad of her thumb. "I think I can get used to it." His eyes smiled at her.

"After this morning, I feel at a disadvantage," she said.

"Oh?"

"You know more about me than I do about you."

His gaze dropped to his soup as he expertly scooped up a dollop of it from the side before it could drip onto the place mat.

"I mean, did you always want to work in the auto industry? I can see a little boy dreaming of growing up to be a race-car driver, or even fixing up classics, but…"

"But you can't imagine a ten-year-old thinking, 'Gee, I think I'll sell car parts when I grow up.'"

He loved it when she smiled.

Drew had to remind himself to eat his soup as he watched the woman across from him. It wasn't that the soup wasn't delicious; it was. It was just that Josie looked even more appetizing.

He'd thought deeply about not coming to the late lunch. But when the time came and went, and the prospect of standing her up became more fact than possibility, he'd found himself almost running in order to make it back to the hotel.

The thought of hurting this beautiful creature, of giving her cause to think he wasn't interested in her, emerged too much of an injustice to ignore.

And now as he sat there enjoying watching her, all misgivings disappeared.

Even her question about his career slid off his back with ease.

And he knew why. His physical need for her

was increasing exponentially with each time their paths crossed, banning his mind from playing any role in what was happening between them on a primal level.

He also knew there was an answer to his dilemma. He could tell her the truth.

6

"No, I DIDN'T DREAM OF BEING a car-parts sales-man." Drew searched for the words to tell her the truth. Tell her who he was and what his intentions were—his client and the consequences be damned. He had to tell her. He couldn't continue without her knowing the truth.

"What did you dream of being?"

The question took Drew aback.

He could count on one hand the times he'd been asked something so personal. And even then the questions had been asked by people like school guidance counselors whose job it was to steer him toward something more productive than what his upbringing had prepared him for.

He looked at Josie now.

"I don't know," he answered honestly.

"There had to be something. A fireman? Police-man?"

"Indian chief?"

Her laugh reached in and touched something he hadn't known was inside him. A sensitive place, a soft spot that absorbed her interest like a dry sponge drank up a drop of water.

"Funny. You know what I mean."

And, remarkably, he did.

Had anyone else asked the question, he would have come up with some off-the cuff response like "A lawyer, because I used to watch Perry Mason."

But he was finding that giving Josie any kind of easy, superficial response was impossible. And that he genuinely wanted to answer her questions.

"A postman."

One of her finely shaped brows rose. "Like in mailman?"

"One and the same." He finished his soup and took a sip of his wine. "Our mailman, George, was just about the only positive male influence I had in my life growing up. So I wanted to be like him." He chuckled quietly, having long forgotten about George and the memories connected to him. "When I was seven I actually went and collected the mail from the neighbors' boxes, put them in my own makeshift bag, then redelivered the mail."

"Oh, boy," Josie said.

"Oh, boy is right. A grumpy old man a couple of trailers up called the police on me. Who knew playing—although *tampering* is the word that was used—with the U.S. mail is a felony?" He shook his head. "The officer that responded seemed to understand, though. He ruffled my hair—which, of course, I hated. George never ruffled my hair. And he told me to go play kick ball or something else that didn't involve the mail. Or if I felt the need to deliver, I could make up my own mail."

"Did you?"

"No. By then the shine was off the silverware."

Josie leaned forward, placing her hands on the table. "You know, listening to you makes me remember about how I once dreamed of being an actress." She cringed as if the memory were embarrassing. "I'd watched a movie with Mae West in it, then found an old red boa in my *granme's* things and proceeded to strut around the hotel flipping the boa and asking, 'Why don't you come up sometime and see me, big boy?'"

"Uh-oh…"

Drew looked around him, considering the type of clientele the hotel attracted.

Josie laughed. "My *granme* nearly strangled me with the boa when she caught a traveling salesman trying to take me up on my offer." She visibly shuddered then smoothed the goose bumps from her arms by rubbing them. "Of course, I was six and had no idea what kind of trouble I could have gotten into if not for my grandmother, but now…"

Drew tried to imagine a six-year-old Josie slinking around the hotel lobby wearing a red boa and making dangerous propositions to strange men. And he felt a desire to protect her surge up within him that he didn't quite know what to do with.

"Oh! I almost forgot the next course."

Drew watched her clear the bowls of soup. "You mean there's more?"

"Is there ever." She took the top off a large pot. Steam rose up, dampening her honey-colored skin and pinkening her cheeks. "Move the silverware and the glasses off to the side of the table for me, will you?"

He did as asked, watching as she tipped a high container full of something he couldn't see into the pot, then used a long-handled spoon to stir the mix. Then she turned and grabbed a small pile of newspapers.

"Here," she said, "help me spread these across the cutting board."

He wasn't sure what she meant, so he watched her open the papers and place them so they covered the surface before him. He did the same. Their hands bumped and they both paused, their gazes meeting between the short distance that separated them.

Up this close, her eyes were the palest shade of brown he'd ever seen. And were so damn captivating he didn't dare blink.

She gave a shaky smile. "I think that should do it."

Was it him or was her voice just a tad breathless?

She went to the pot and lifted what looked like a colander from inside it. Giving it a good shake, she stepped to the table then tipped the contents out onto the papers.

Crabs. Dozens of them. Orange and glistening and all about the size of his hand.

She put the colander back inside the pot then returned to the table, handing him what looked like a nutcracker.

"Blue crabs," she said. "A Creole specialty. Although they're better in the spring during the mating season, these will do." She gestured to where he held his shell cracker awkwardly. "You probably won't need those since the shells are soft."

Drew chuckled, staring at the mass of seafood covering the papers between them. "What do I do?"

She picked up one of the crabs then inserted her fingertips into the top and pulled. The shell easily split in two. She picked meat out and slipped it into her mouth, moaning as she licked her fingers. "Try it."

He did and found it amazingly easy to mimic her movements.

"No, don't eat that," she said. "Intestines." She gestured toward the top half. "There."

He carefully plucked out the meat and put it into his mouth. The texture was smooth and solid and magnificently good. The flavor exploded on Drew's tongue. "Spicy."

She smiled. "It's the boil."

He opened another crab.

"Mmm, a sook." Josie leaned across the table and scooped something out near the bottom of the inner shell. "Here," she murmured, holding the food near his mouth.

His heart beating thickly in his chest, he leaned forward and opened his mouth, slowly encircling her slender fingers with it. He closed his lips, enjoying the taste of the crab as much as the taste of her. Hot cayenne pepper and sweet Josie was a combination no man could resist. And Drew wasn't in a resistant mood.

He sucked gently, then swirled his tongue around her index finger, his gaze glued to her expressive face. The black of her pupils nearly overtook the golden brown of her irises and she caught her breath as he trailed his own damp fingertips over the inside of her wrist.

"Those, um, are the female's eggs."

He withdrew his mouth. "Good thing you told me that after I ate them."

She sat back down. "Best part of the crab."

They ate in silence for the next few minutes, although Drew's mind couldn't have been farther from the food in front of him, no matter how good. Instead, his thoughts were solely on the delicious woman across from him.

Damn, but she was beautiful. And sexy. And the seductive way she cracked open the small crab claws and sucked the meat from them made his groin pull tight. What made him harder still was the unselfconscious way she ate, without concern of how she might appear, no pretense, no formalities. Only a pure enjoyment of the meal and of his company.

He hadn't realized he'd stopped eating until her movements slowed, then halted altogether. Her mouth was slightly open, as if she couldn't pull in enough air from her nose alone. And he felt like the precious resource was at a premium in the warm room. He watched her pulse beat at the base of her throat, a droplet of moisture moving down her neck to disappear into the deep neckline of her dress. He followed the movement and unconsciously licked the corner of his mouth as if he could taste the salty droplet.

Josie's pulse pounded so hard she couldn't hear anything else but the hastening beat of her heart. As Drew's gaze slid to her breasts, she felt her nipples harden into tight knots beneath the light fabric covering them. He looked devilishly handsome in that one moment. Irresistible. And so damn sexy that she felt her mouth water with the desire to kiss him again. Not on a public street. But here in the private haven of her hotel's kitchen.

At the same time, they reached for the newspapers covering the cutting board between them, shoving them and the shells and whole crabs to the floor along with their wineglasses and the bottle of wine. They both climbed up on top, their hands seeking each other's faces, their mouths meeting hungrily.

Josie couldn't remember a time when she'd been so spontaneously compelled to have sex with anyone before. She wanted Drew with an urgency that almost hurt.

He touched her legs, scooting his fingers up the hem where she kneeled. When she thought he might touch her aching flesh, he rounded to her panty-covered bottom and pulled her until she was straddling him on top of the table. She snaked her arms around his neck and held tight, feeling the rigid length of him nestled in her shallow channel, nothing but fabric separating them. She restlessly tilted her head to the right, then the left, kissing him with a desperation that bordered on insanity, as he did the same with her, first holding her head still as he launched an assault on her lips, then pulling her hips tightly against his until she moaned.

"Jesus," he ground out, nuzzling her neck almost roughly. "I'm burning up."

She threaded her fingers through his hair, mindless that they were still damp with crab juice, and kissed him. "It's the spices."

He shook his head as they kissed again. "No, Josie, it's you."

He peeled her from him then slid off the table, pulling her hips until they were even with the edge. Josie gasped at the sudden move, helpless to stop him as he shoved her dress up. Her chest heaved as he stared at her womanhood covered by her purple satin panties. She pulled the rest of the dress off, watching with satisfaction as his gaze moved from her thighs to her breasts. Breasts that were normally constrained in a bra but she'd left free and loose while she cooked.

He leaned in as if to take one of her breasts into his mouth, but she stilled him with a hand against his chest, then pulled his shirt up and over his head. She took him in. For a car-parts salesman, he had a dark tan and a fit physique, equal to that of a male cover model. She licked her finger and drew it from his thick, well-defined collarbone down around one of his flat nipples, before tweaking the tiny pebble of flesh then drawing it into her mouth.

Drew grew taut, groaning at her unexpected attention. It seemed only natural to Josie that if a woman could get so much pleasure from having her breasts licked, then the same would apply to a man. And she took private pleasure in being proven right.

Drew's fingers dug into the soft flesh of her thighs as she worked, laving each of his nipples then suckling them, blowing on the distended flesh while it was still wet. His hips bucked, putting his erection against her. Then his fingers found the sides of her panties and he stepped back, freeing her from her one last bit of clothing.

He stood for long moments, saying nothing as he nudged her knees farther apart with his hips and stood gazing at her bared womanhood with what she could only call awe. Then he was touching her dark, springy curls, parting her farther. Josie grasped his shoulders and shivered at his light touch.

He kissed her again. Hard and demandingly. Slowly, almost imperceptibly, he pushed her back until she lay flat against the table. He rested one hand between her breasts and held her still as he leaned forward to pull one of her nipples deep into mouth.

Sensation exploded within Josie. Hot, so very hot. Realization slowly sank through her passion-clouded mind that it must be the spices. The cayenne they'd eaten and that remained on Drew's tongue made each lick hotter than the one before, adding a sensation she'd never experienced before. She tightly grasped his shoulders, bracing herself as a blissful shudder ran through her body.

Is that how her licking had made him feel?

She didn't have a chance to answer the question because Drew had left her breasts and was laving a path down her quivering stomach toward the V of black hair at the top of her thighs. She restlessly licked her lips, wondering if her sensitive flesh could withstand the spicy attention. Then he was parting her with his thumbs and taking her tight bud between his lips and the worry was whipped from her mind, replaced by searing pleasure.

"Oh!" Josie sought something, anything, to grab a hold of—Drew's hair, the edge of the table—to gain a stability that she feared she'd never find again. He sucked in deeply, then one of his fingers rimmed her flesh before thrusting inside to the hilt, so that she felt the palm of his hand pressing against her burning clit.

Red, hot sensation shot over and through and around Josie again and again. She writhed on the table, bearing down against the hand bringing her so much pleasure, rubbing the spices even farther into her swollen flesh.

She was just beginning to flutter back down to earth when she blinked open her eyes to find Drew had shucked his pants with his free hand and was rolling a condom down the thick, hard length of his erection. She swallowed hard and braced her feet against the side of the table, readying herself for his first thrust.

7

NEVER HAD DREW VIEWED a sight as breath-stealing as Josie spilled over the cutting-board table, her X-rated body undulating in pleasure as she welcomed the climax he'd brought her to. And now as she readied herself for him, he wondered if he'd ever made love to a woman so gloriously unconscious of the way she looked. A woman not driven by shallow motivations but by a deeper need to connect with him in the way he needed to connect with her.

Drew touched her feet, caressing his way up her silky legs to her knees, his gaze caught by hers. Forgotten was the fact that they were in the kitchen of a hotel. Gone were any concerns over his role in her life. All that mattered was this one moment in time.

He positioned his hard-on between her slick, fleshy lips and rubbed himself lengthwise down then up again, purposely denying himself the pleasure of filling her as he stroked her externally.

He watched her throw back her head as if the anticipation were killing her. She tried to force a breach by curving her ankles around his waist and drawing him against her. But the urgency of her movements merely increased his desire to draw this out.

He worked his head against her clit, massaging it, the catch in her breath and the shivering of her stomach revealing the effect he was having on her.

An effect that mirrored the quake beginning to shake him from the inside out.

He couldn't remember a time when he'd felt so…at one with a woman. So on the same wavelength. He didn't need to hurry. Or wonder if he was doing the right thing. Or listen to her whisper orders about how to touch her there or do this just so. Instead there existed a mutual understanding between them that all was game and that the simplest touch could be the most erotic. There was no rushing toward an end.

Finally, Drew fit the thick, pulsating head of his erection against her opening. He paused, noticing the way she stopped breathing, her face flushed, her lips parted as she anticipated his next move. He slowly entered her by degrees then stopped, allowing her tight, slick muscles to become acclimated to his girth. She hungrily licked her lips, allowing him to call the shots. Drew reveled in the power he had. Over himself. Over her. Over them both.

He glided in to the hilt, the quake inside shaking him to the core while Josie's moan wove around him. Her back arched and her glistening breasts shivered. Drew felt as if his very heart beat at the base of his penis as he slowly withdrew then stroked her again…and again.

Josie released her ankles and matched his deep rhythm, her eyelids fluttering closed with every thrust as if unable to bear the exquisite pleasure that he was giving her. That they were experiencing together.

He splayed his hands against her stomach, wondering at the narrowness of her waist, the fullness of her breasts, the dark rose of her puckered nipples. The moisture that clung to her skin made her look darker yet. Keeping his strokes long and deep, he slowly slid his fingers down over her sides, then back up and over her breasts, intoxicated by the feel of her inside and out.

He realized he'd stopped his movements, his erection throbbing inside her. He watched her suck her bottom lip into her mouth and bite down hard as if unable to take the torture. Drew slipped his hands to her hips and held her tight as he withdrew then thrust into her hard.

"Yes. Oh, dear God, yes…"

Her softly whispered words empowered him further and he increased the speed of his thrusts, the next faster and harder than the one before. He wanted to consume her. Wanted to possess every part of her. The sound of damp, hard flesh smacking together filled his ears: the sweet smell of her sex blended with his sex filled his nose.

Then he was sailing over the edge of the world and into a parallel universe he'd never visited before, suspended in darkness, his mind uncharacteristically unconcerned about his powerless state.

Then Josie cried out, in the middle of her own crisis and he was moving again. Frenetically, wildly, speeding through the darkness with an incredible sense of freedom.

LATER THAT NIGHT, as Josie sat at the quiet front desk, darkness having long since fallen outside the open doors, she trembled just thinking about what had passed between her and Drew in the kitchen.

She wished it could have continued, that they could have gone upstairs to his room and explored each other well into the night, but Philippe couldn't stay because of an appointment he had to take his mother to. Even so, Josie didn't have the money to pay him overtime.

At any rate, Drew had a reception party of some sort he needed to attend at the convention hotel. His immediate superior would be going and would expect to see him there. So she sat at the front desk alone, unable to wipe the wistful smile from her face. She couldn't even bring herself to care about the debts she couldn't cover or the future of the hotel. Both concerns would still be there in the morning, she told herself.

Right now…well, right now, she wanted to enjoy the blissful aftermath of great sex.

A sound from upstairs drew her attention.

Josie's hand froze at her neck as her gaze swept toward the steps. With Drew out for the evening and Philippe gone, no one was in the hotel but her.

She was probably imagining things. Either that, or the light breeze had stirred something from its resting place.

Another noise.

Okay, maybe she wasn't imagining things.

She rose from the chair and looked toward the open front doors and the tourists passing by in a colorful stream. No one seemed to be interested in her or the Josephine.

The unmistakable sound of footsteps overhead.

Here and there since the passing of her *granme* she'd thought she'd heard sounds. Had even imagined that her grandmother had found a way to stay around for a bit to watch out for her. The sensation had been so intense on occasion that Josie could have sworn she felt a hand on her shoulder or a brush against her temple.

But this didn't feel like that. This felt…different.

Josie steeled herself, considering her options. She strode to close both doors, then stepped back behind the desk and took out the sawed-off shotgun she had locked in a compartment there. The firearm had been there for as long as she could remember. Certainly longer than Josie had been part of the hotel.

She climbed the stairs, having long memorized which creaked where and avoiding those spots. She emerged onto the second floor, the scent of sulfur assaulting her nose.

Oh, God. Something was burning.

She went to the door to Room 2C, Drew's room, and used her master key to open the door. Nothing. No lights were on. Only the sound of the light sheers at the open doors flapping slightly in the warm breeze.

She backtracked out into the hall and went to 2B

next door. Again, she opened the lock with her master key and peered inside. No one and nothing in sight.

She stepped to the closed door to 2D, her heart thudding heavily in her chest.

This was the room Claire Laraway was killed in just over two weeks ago. And forever in the back of her mind was the fact that her killer had yet to be caught.

Gripping the shotgun tightly in her right hand, she tried to manipulate the master key with her left. After two tries, she finally swung the door inward so that it crashed against the inside wall. She aimed the gun straight in front of her, ready to protect herself against any threat.

The source of the sulfur smell became immediately apparent. She stared at the wrought-iron bed where Claire had lain, her beautiful neck slit. In the middle sat a dozen lit black candles, their flames flickering in the cross draught she'd created by opening the door.

She slowly turned to her right, pointing the end of the shotgun in the direction of her gaze. No one was in there. She checked the connecting bathroom, with the same result.

But that was impossible. Someone had to have set up the candles, lit them and made the sounds she'd heard. She quickly blew out the candles then backtracked to the hall.

There were two ways to access the hall, from the lobby steps she'd used to come up, and from stairs leading to the kitchen. She took those now, careful to keep the gun out in front of her. While she'd never shot at anyone, she wasn't adverse to it if the situation called for it.

She emerged into the dim kitchen. Only the light above the large industrial stove was on.

And the back door, the same door she had bolted before going to look after the front desk, was hanging wide open, the screen door budging back and forth as if just used...

Drew tried the front doors to the hotel. They were locked.

He stepped back and looked over the hotel. That was strange. Why would the doors be locked?

He rapped lightly on the glass, trying to see inside.

The right door swung suddenly inward and there stood Josie looking pale and holding what looked like a modified shotgun.

"Jesus Christ, what happened?" He took the firearm from her and strode into the lobby, looking around for the person who had put the disturbing expression on Josie's face and the gun in her hands.

She shook her head. "They're gone."

She held out her hand for the gun and he gave

it back to her. She stepped behind the desk and put it away into a locked compartment.

"Who's gone?" he asked, moving to the other side of the desk.

"Whoever set the ritual altar in 2D."

He wasn't following her.

She sighed and smoothed the back of her shaking hand across her forehead. While she obviously wanted to make him think she was all right, he'd like to think he'd come to know her better than that.

Damn it, he should never have left her alone earlier.

But their session in the kitchen had been so intense, so raw, that he'd needed to get out to think a bit. To convince himself he was imagining the connection that he feared was forming between them.

And when that didn't work, to consider where they went from there.

"What do you mean, altar? Have you called the police?"

She shook her head. "No."

"Why the hell not?" He pulled the phone closer to him on the desk and picked up the receiver.

She punched down the disconnect button. "Don't."

"Why not? Obviously someone who wasn't supposed to be in here was and did something they shouldn't. If that doesn't demand a police report, I don't know what does."

"I don't need the publicity."

"Publicity, my ass, Josie." He removed her hand and dialed 911.

Moments later he hung up. "They'll be here in half an hour to an hour."

She smiled faintly then sat in the chair behind the desk. "You don't understand. This wasn't so much a crime as it was a warning."

"Show me."

Five minutes later, Drew stood staring at the myriad black candles in the middle of the bed in 2D. Small satchels were lain in front of them and black wax had trickled over to pool on the white coverlet. He tried the switch for the overhead lights, but it didn't work.

"Isn't this where the girl was killed?" he asked.

She blinked at him.

"Your maid likes to gossip," he told her, although he knew about the killing because he knew a lot more than a regular guest would.

She nodded and crossed her arms over her chest.

As they stood staring at each other, it was hard to believe that only a few short hours earlier they'd been joined together in ecstasy. That he'd spread her out on top of the cutting board in the kitchen and made love to her in a way he'd never made love to a woman before.

He stepped closer to her, brushing back a dark curl from her cheek.

"Are you okay?" he asked quietly.

He hadn't thought of asking her before, if only because some sort of primal need to protect her had kicked in. But now that the danger had passed and the police were on their way, he focused on the woman in front of him.

She laughed quietly and as far as he could tell there was no fear in the sound, no anxiety. Merely a soft edge. "I'm fine."

She turned from him and went to open the double doors to the connecting balcony.

"What do you mean this was meant as a warning?" he asked.

"Just what I said. This—" she gestured toward the bed "—is a curse of sorts."

"Voodoo?"

"Black magic."

She led the way from the room and back down to the front desk. Drew followed.

"Explain the difference."

"Voodoo can be either black or white magic. It can be used for bad or good."

"And in this case it was used for bad."

She nodded.

"Do you have any idea who'd want to do this?"

She didn't answer right away as she fooled around with things on the desk.

"Josie?"

She shrugged her slender shoulders. "I'll take care of it."

Drew opened his mouth to object, then realized there was no objection for him to make. He'd had sex with her. Nothing more, nothing less. He was a temporary guest in her hotel in the middle of one of the most decadent cities in the world. And, as she'd told him during their walk earlier, it was all temporary. Tomorrow didn't exist. At least not where they were concerned.

And that, suddenly, was unacceptable to him.

8

"HOLY MOTHER OF GOD," Josie heard Monique say as the maid rushed down the stairs into the lobby the following morning, crossing herself countless times before looking at Josie with eyes the size of large, glossy marbles. "You got the voodoo."

Josie stretched her neck. She'd forgotten to tell Monique not to bother with Room 2D, that she'd see to cleaning up the mess in there herself, but hadn't had a chance after Philippe had called in sick, leaving her alone to man the desk. Something he must have eaten, he'd said, saying he'd try to make it in later if he felt better.

Now she stood staring at a clearly terrified Monique.

Josie had been raised around voodoo. It was as much a part of her heritage as her dark, Caribbean skin. While her *granme* had never practiced it or let her anywhere near it growing up, she remembered her mother trying out love spells in an attempt to get the latest true love to fall for her and take her away from this life.

Josie had never placed much stock in the hokey rituals. Oh, she knew enough about them. Even counted priests and priestesses among her friends, including her best friend, Anne-Marie Paré, and the Rooster Man, the old black man who lived up the block and whose counsel many sought to lift curses and perform white magic spells. It was said that back in the day, the Rooster Man had placed his share of curses. But it was also said that for every bad spell that was cast, bad luck to the power of ten would return to the caster. When his wife and young son were killed in a freak automobile accident thirty years ago, he'd done a one-eighty and only performed good voodoo. Some said he performed white magic as penance for past wrongs and to guarantee his family entrance into heaven.

Josie thought it was more likely the only way he knew how to make a living and that he had long since stopped believing in any higher spiritual power.

"Monique, Monique, get yourself together, girl." She rounded the desk and pried the broom from the young woman's hands before she broke the stick and hurt herself. "I'll take care of 2D."

She touched Monique's arm to find her cold. "In fact, why don't you go ahead and take the day off altogether? I'll take care of the duties."

Monique nodded several times. "Yes, yes. I need to make sure that nothing sticks to me."

Josie knew what she meant. She wanted to make certain that the curse meant for Josie hadn't transferred to her.

She watched Monique hightail it out of the hotel without another backward glance. What remained was who would want to place a curse on her in the first place. She remembered Drew asking the question last night. Who would want to do this? She hadn't told him. Mostly because she didn't want to speak ill of anyone unless she was entirely sure they were behind it. But also partly because she had been too tempted to melt into Drew's ready arms and let him take care of her.

The temptation itself had frightened her more than the voodoo ritual. She'd never allowed anyone to take care of her. Mostly because there had never been anyone who had offered to take the job. Even her *granme* had warned her from a young age, "You've got to learn how to step up and take care of yourself, Josephine." Usually these words came after she'd been frightened by something and had turned to her grandmother for comfort.

She would give it to her, but in small doses. "Ain't nobody going to take care of you as well as you can take care of yourself. And I'm not going to be here forever."

Josie looked toward an undefined spot above herself, wondering at the prophetic content of her grandmother's words.

The police had come and gone last night, barely making note of the event except for its connection to the murder of the girl. Fact was, voodoo rituals were more the norm than the exception in New Orleans, and if the police followed up on every reported voodoo spell, the city's crime rate would raise exponentially because they wouldn't have time to do anything else. Voodoo shops selling do-it-yourself ritual kits were everywhere in the Quarter. On occasion, Josie herself had even browsed through a shop or two, curious. And, of course, Anne-Marie owned one where she also consulted tarot cards and gave spiritual readings. Before her grandmother had passed away, when Josie had had the time and cash for outings, she'd often met Anne-Marie there and they'd gone out for lunch. And now and then Anne-Marie had even set up shop here in the hotel's courtyard.

Interestingly enough, her friend really hadn't

been by since *Granme* had passed, except to pay her respects. Even then, she'd commented on some sort of "presence" in the hotel and had appeared uncomfortable.

There was a shadow at the door. Josie turned toward it, her heart giving a squeeze as she found herself wishing it were Drew. Only it wasn't. Instead, it was a man she was hoping to avoid by not calling the police last night.

"Detective Chevalier," she greeted coolly, pretending an interest in her nearly empty guest book on the desk.

"Miss Villefranche." He took off his fedora and put it on the desk on top of the book, forcing her gaze up to him.

N.O. Homicide Detective Alan Chevalier had worked the case of Claire Laraway and, if his presence was any indication, he still was.

"I heard about what happened last night," he said. "Any idea who might want to do something like that?"

She shrugged, removed the book from under his hat and then closed it. "Probably some neighborhood kids playing a prank."

And the phone calls? she silently asked. *Were those a prank, as well?*

"Hmm. Have you cleaned up yet?"

She turned and retrieved the key for 2D. "No. Make yourself at home."

He stared at her for a long moment, then took the key.

"Don't mind if I do." He looked around the empty lobby. "How many guests do you have in residence?"

Josie's throat tightened. "One."

His brows rose.

While the Josephine had never been a popular place, she had managed to keep at least half her rooms full most times.

Most times, that is, until the unsolved murder two weeks ago.

"Who?"

"A businessman in for a convention," she said, hating to describe Drew that way. "A Mr. Drew Morrison."

"Is he in?"

She shook her head.

"Well, I'll be wanting to talk to him."

"He wasn't here when I found the candles."

"Nonetheless…"

He left the word hanging as he turned to make his way toward the steps. Halfway there, he backtracked and picked up his hat, folding the brim back as he looked at her. Then he turned away again.

"Detective?" she found herself saying as he climbed the first couple of stairs.

He slowed his steps then stopped, apparently waiting for her to continue.

Josie swallowed hard, realizing she had nearly told him of the late-night phone calls.

"Would you like something to drink? A tea, perhaps?"

"Yes. I'd like that. I'll take it in the courtyard when I'm done."

DREW STOOD AT THE PAY PHONE in Jackson Square waiting to be put through to his client. He watched people pass, some natives, most tourists, then glanced toward Bourbon Street a couple blocks up from where Hotel Josephine was located. He hadn't slept well last night. He couldn't get his mind off what had happened after he'd left, but more importantly, what had occurred after his return.

Josie didn't trust him. He knew it wasn't because he'd tipped his hand. Rather, Josie seemed to be naturally wary of letting anyone too close. He supposed that was due in part to the strong women in her family. As far as he could tell, the past four generations of Villefranche women had had no men in their lives. They'd been fiercely independent and it was only natural that Josie had inherited that trait.

But that made his job all the more difficult.

His client finally came on the line.

"Hello, Morrison," he said.

Drew got straight to the point. "Who else you got working this case?"

Silence, then, "What makes you ask that?"

"Just answer the question."

Nothing.

"Look, the person is making my job next to impossible and is only guaranteeing Josie Villefranche won't sell."

"More's the pity."

Drew let loose a series of curses after putting his hand over the receiver.

"Morrison, we don't have anyone else on the case."

His movements stilled.

If there was no one else working the case, then that meant the happenings last night had nothing to do with forcing Josie to sell and everything to do with scaring her.

"Close the deal, Morrison. You have three days."

Drew hung up the phone then rubbed his hand over the back of his neck. Three days. Such a short time. But if he didn't make the deadline, he wouldn't get paid.

And, more importantly, he wouldn't get a shot at the next contract he wanted.

He strode purposefully down toward Bourbon Street and the hotel.

DUE TO ALL THE ACTIVITY, Josie hadn't had a chance to distribute the Stay One Night, Get One Night Free coupons she'd made up. She stood at the front desk, fingering the slips of paper, trying to ignore that ten minutes ago a couple of police crime-scene investigators had quietly come in and joined Detective Chevalier upstairs. Philippe had yet to show and she was worried about him.

And Drew...

She took a deep breath and placed the coupons under the desk where she could easily access them later. Drew was an unknown quantity she really didn't have the time to consider now. Sure, she'd had mind-blowing sex with him, but she'd gone into it knowing that there was no future beyond that moment. And now that the future had arrived in all its frightening glory, her mind needed to be on the matter at hand, not remembering the way it had felt to have Drew's mouth slide down over her shoulder, dampening her skin and igniting nerve endings that seemed to lead straight between her legs.

She picked up her *granme*'s hand fan and

waved it in front of her flushed face as she sat down, watching the current of people move past her front door without a glance her way.

There were times throughout her life when she'd sat just as she was now, watching the people walk by and feeling like she was being left behind somehow. Like each person represented the ticking of a clock. There went an hour. Six hours. A day.

Usually it didn't bother her much, the sensation of standing still while time marched on. But lately she'd begun to know a tinge of restlessness. Was she doing what she wanted to be doing? Was marriage something she was even remotely interested in? Did she want a child?

The questions lurked beneath the surface and chose times like these to rise and haunt her.

She'd never really considered the child question seriously. Sure, she'd had her collection of dolls when she was a girl, but given her connection to the hotel, she'd never been around children much. Besides, since hitting puberty, the focus had been on not getting pregnant and "ending up like her mother, stuck with a kid to raise and no man around to help." Her *granme* had never said anything along those lines; her mother had, but her grandmother had strongly cautioned her to avoid pregnancy. Getting knocked up had been ranked right up there with driving drunk or taking drugs.

Still, did she want at least one child of her own?

And if she did, what were her options except to raise it herself, alone, without the help of a man?

Drew came to mind and she closed her eyes as much to banish the image as cherish it.

What did it matter anyway? The way things stood right now, she wouldn't be able to take care of *herself* financially. To even consider adding a child to the mix was ridiculous and irresponsible and the ultimate in selfishness.

Footsteps on the lobby floor.

"Uh-huh. The rumors are right," her friend Anne-Marie said, looking warily around the lobby. "You got the voodoo but good."

9

DREW HAD WANTED TO MAKE a beeline straight for Josie when he'd returned to the hotel, but was thwarted by the presence of a woman who had to be around Josie's age but looked at least thirty years older. It was more than the colorful turban and the loose-fitting long dress. Her haunted eyes were older than her years.

Josie sat with the dark woman in the courtyard, tiny coffee cups between them, the other woman's many bracelets jangling as she gestured with her hands while she spoke. Josie sat back, seeming amused by what her companion had to say, but also paying attention.

Drew stepped into the courtyard.

Josie looked at him, and the woman she was with studied him with a guarded expression.

"Drew," Josie greeted.

"Sorry, I didn't mean to interrupt."

"Come. I'd like you to meet an old friend of

mine. Anne-Marie Paré, this is Drew Morrison. He's a…guest at the hotel. The only guest actually."

Anne-Marie extended her hand toward him. Drew took it, noticing the cracked red nail polish she wore and the ashy appearance of her skin.

"A pleasure," he said.

"Hmm," Anne-Marie responded, her dark eyes intense as she looked him over. "I'd say Mr. Morrison here is more than a guest."

Josie smiled. "Anne-Marie is a voodoo priestess."

"Ah," Drew said, extracting his hand from the uncanny woman's bony grasp.

"Miss Villefranche?"

Josie looked over his shoulder to where a man stood wearing a wrinkled gray trench coat and holding a fedora.

"Detective Chevalier."

"Do you have a moment?"

Josie excused herself, leaving Drew with Anne-Marie and her unsettling eyes.

"Please," she said, indicating the chair across from her with a jangling motion of her hand. "Sit."

"I'm GOING TO GO NOW," Chevalier told Josie. "But my men will be upstairs for a little while longer."

"Fine."

He regarded the small notebook he held and squinted at her. "Is there anything else you'd like to add to what the responding police officer reported last night?"

Josie dropped her gaze then shook her head.

"No unusual characters hanging around?"

"No."

"It says here you heard sounds?"

"Yes. And when I came back downstairs after investigating—" she left out that she'd had her unregistered, illegal sawed-off shotgun with her "—I found the back door to the alley open when I had already closed and locked it for the night."

Alan made a check mark on his pad. "Okay. I guess that's all for now."

It was far from all, but Josie didn't know what else she could do—until she thought to ask a few questions of her own. "Do you think the incident is connected to the murder?"

Chevalier looked at her. "That's what we're trying to figure out."

She looked toward the stairs, remembering the morning two weeks earlier when Monique had found the body in the same room where the ritual had been performed. "Has any progress been made on finding the killer?"

She hoped an arrest of the murderer would set things back to right and send customers her way.

"No." He didn't look pleased.

Seeing as Josie didn't feel pleased, she figured they were even.

He handed her a business card, a twin of which she had tucked in a drawer somewhere from their earlier encounter. "When your guest Mr. Morrison returns, tell him to give me a call."

Josie resisted the urge to look into the courtyard where the man in question was now sitting with Anne-Marie.

"I will," she said instead.

He began walking toward the door.

"Detective?"

He turned around.

"A rain check on that tea?"

For what had to be the first time since they'd met over two weeks ago, he cracked a smile. Surprisingly, the expression made him look younger and almost attractive. "I just might take you up on that."

FOR THE NEXT TWENTY MINUTES, Josie hung on the fringes of the courtyard, listening in on Anne-Marie's conversation with Drew. Although it wasn't a conversation, really. Rather, Anne-Marie had taken out her ever-present tarot cards and was doing a reading for Drew. He looked to be taking it all in stride, although there appeared to be a bit of tension around his handsome mouth.

At one point, he caught Josie's gaze. She half expected him to give her a "help me" look, but instead he grinned at her as if just seeing her made him happy.

"You're not what you appear to be, are you, Mr. Morrison?"

Anne-Marie made the declaration, snapping both Josie's and Drew's attention back to her.

"Pardon me?"

Josie identified the tower card Anne-Marie had just turned over across the knight of swords. "Mystery shrouds you and your intentions aren't what you make them out to be."

Drew blinked.

"That's enough for today," Josie said, stepping to the table and turning over Anne-Marie's cards, then handing them back to her.

Her friend appeared none too happy. "Now look what you've gone and done, girl. You've messed with my mojo."

Hojo, mojo, Josie thought. Just as she'd never put much stock in the voodoo rituals, she didn't read much into Anne-Marie's visions, either, whether they were conjured from her tarot cards or from out of thin air. If you could see it and touch it and smell it, then it was real. Otherwise, it was all a bunch of hokey BS.

"That's all right," Drew said, surprising her. "I'm curious to hear what your friend has to say."

Anne-Marie had encircled her hands as Josie had tried to give her the cards and now the voodoo priestess stared at her hard, as if trying to see beyond Josie's intentions.

Anne-Marie finally blinked, then released her hands. "No, no. Josie is right. I've said far too much already." She gathered the remainder of her cards then slid them into the small, red velvet pouch she kept them in.

Drew rose at the same time as his tablemate. "It was a pleasure making your acquaintance, Miss Paré."

Anne-Marie extended her hand and allowed Drew to give it a polite shake.

HOURS LATER, BACK IN HIS ROOM, Drew sat on his bed with his briefcase open, reading some papers. He'd already done most of the preliminary investigating for the job he wanted next.

He sat back on the bed, the springs giving a low squeak. As hard as he tried to concentrate, his mind kept going back to what the tarot-card reader had said: "You're not what you appear to be, are you, Mr. Morrison?"

That was all right. He supposed that many people in her profession used the same line. It could apply to everyone who had ever told a white lie, much less a black one, at any point in their lives.

But the follow-up comment about mystery shrouding him and his intentions not being what he made them out to be had struck home with an accuracy that left him wanting to explain himself.

Though justifying his actions was becoming less and less a possibility.

The sound of a trumpet playing a bluesy tune drifted on the hot air from the open doors. He dropped the papers in his briefcase and stepped to the balcony, watching a black man in a multicolored knit cap playing solo on the corner, most of the passersby ignoring the case spread at his feet for change. Not that the player noticed. He appeared to be playing for himself, no one else. At one with his instrument, which gleamed in the dim light from the street lamp.

Then his eyes opened and he seemed to be looking directly at Drew, even though he stood well in the shadows and a constant herd of people was walking by in front of him.

Drew backed up farther into the hotel room, a

strange feeling of being exposed filling his gut. He ran his fingers through his hair. But that was ridiculous. Just as there was no way Anne-Marie could know the true nature of his visit to the city and to Hotel Josephine, surely no street performer could identify him and his reason for being there.

"He's blind."

Drew turned around to find Josie standing behind him.

She blinked, apparently seeing something in his eyes that startled her.

"I'm sorry. I knocked, but you didn't answer. And the door was unlocked."

Foolish of him.

Even more foolish was the way he wanted to envelop her in his arms.

"Who's blind?"

She gestured toward the street. "The trumpet player. Clarence has been blind all his life."

If the man was blind, then there was no way he could have been looking at Drew.

Just the same, Drew sensed that not only had he been spotted, but also that he'd been seen. The same way Anne-Marie had seemed to see him.

The same way Josie saw him now.

He found it difficult to swallow as his gaze swept over her beautiful face.

Damn, but the woman did strange, unfamiliar things to him. The instant she came into view, everything else disappeared, leaving only her and him.

His desire for her was so strong it seemed able to bridge whatever gap lay between them. Only there was no gap between them now, at least not physically. She stood near enough to touch. And he wanted to touch her with an intensity that set him off balance.

"Is Philippe watching the desk?"

Josie's gaze lingered on his mouth. "Philippe never made it in today. Sick." She licked her lips, her eyes shifting to look into his. "I put the Closed sign out."

He remembered hearing the sound of other voices a little earlier. "Are we the only ones in the hotel?"

She slowly shook her head. "No. Frederique came back with another…friend. I, um, told her to close the door when she leaves."

Drew reached out and stroked her silky cheek. "Now that the police are gone, it's back to business as usual?"

"No. I mean, yes, but…"

Drew was as drawn to her as she apparently was to him. He could barely force himself to think of anything or anyone else. Only Josie, and how much he wanted to stroke her amazingly supple body. Lose himself in the feel, smell and touch of her.

She stepped into his arms, her smaller body somehow fitting perfectly against his larger frame. The move chased all air from his lungs. Not because of the impact, but because of her nearness. Up this close, he could smell the subtle scent of night-blooming jasmine that emanated from her skin. Absorb the welcome heat of her body. Feel the way her breasts pressed harder against the wall of his chest with each breath that she took.

She didn't play coy. Didn't ask questions or make nervous comments. She merely acted on an instinct that was purely primal, that made him respond in kind.

Drew smoothed his hands over her slender back then reached to tip her chin up so he could kiss her.

Damn, but she tasted better, sweeter, than anyone he'd ever met before. Like freshly picked fruit. Like cayenne pepper and milk-laced coffee and sugarcoated doughnuts. Like heaven and sin all at once.

The sound of the trumpet continued outside the open doors, and the squeak of bedsprings in the room next to his spoke of their neighbors' activities. All of it a backdrop to the steady thrum of blood through Drew's veins as he kissed the woman in his arms.

And prepared to make love to her for as long as she'd let him.

10

No matter how hard Josie tried, she couldn't seem to draw in a breath deep enough to clear her mind. Then again, air probably had nothing to do with her light-headed state. She suspected Drew was completely responsible for that. The gentle way he held her. The soft, knowing stroke of his hands over her back and her face. The growing hardness against her stomach.

He gripped her chin in his hand and kissed her deeply, stealing the bone from her knees and rendering her helpless to his sensual onslaught.

Yesterday had been all about urgency. By closing the hotel for the first time in its recent history, she'd guaranteed that tonight would be all about slow and sure.

Drew's tongue stroked hers. If she'd harbored any doubts about coming to his room, they all but disappeared. She wanted this. Needed to feel grounded, real, and in control. It was strange that she should feel that when she seemed to have no control over herself the instant Drew touched her.

Everything in her life was spiraling out of control. She stood on the brink of losing her hotel. Someone was taking extreme measures to try to frighten her. And out there somewhere was a killer who could strike again anytime.

Drew's hand rested at the base of her neck, his index finger caressing as if monitoring the quickening of her pulse there. Then he was working that same index finger under the thin strap of her slip dress, doing the same with his hand on her other shoulder, so that the light material whispered down over her breasts and hips and then puddled around her ankles. Josie stepped out of the circle, gloriously aware that she was completely exposed while Drew was fully dressed.

She was about to remedy that when he swept her up and carried her to the bed. Whatever he'd had on top thudded to the floor and then he was laying her down, only momentarily breaking their long, leisurely kiss.

He climbed onto the bed with her, positioning himself between her legs then prying open her knees with a slow nudge. His thigh slid against her throbbing womanhood, causing her back to come up off the mattress. He took full advantage of her momentary distraction and ran his tongue along an engorged nipple before sucking it into his mouth.

The bed beneath Josie was soft and cool, while Drew above her was hard and hot. She reveled in the contrast as he lifted to kiss her again. At the opportunity, she went to work on the buttons of his shirt, tucking her fingers inside the edges so that they brushed against the warm steel of his stomach. She reached the bottom and pressed her palm flat against his abdomen, just above his erection. She savored his low hiss before pushing the material from his wide shoulders. There. She wanted to kiss him there. She placed her lips against his shoulder, swirling her tongue against the salty, manly taste of his skin. And there. She kissed his collarbone. And there…

Everywhere she kissed him left her wanting more.

Drew moved so that both his knees were between hers. He lay against her so that his long, rigid hardness was cradled between her legs. She grasped his hips, holding him there, swimming in the anticipation that shuddered through her.

The slow burn was quickly turning into something more powerful. Josie braced her hands against his shoulders then turned him over so that he was lying on the mattress and she was above him. She kissed him long and hard, her right hand slinking down over his torso toward his slacks. She popped the fastener then tugged down the zipper, dipping her hand inside his boxers so she could cup his silken length. So long…so thick…so hard. She pulled her mouth from his, her breasts swaying as she repositioned herself between his knees. She caught him watching the movement. She grazed her nipples against his chest, first one way, then the other, rubbing them against his. His eyes darkened and he grasped her hips, shoving down her panties to bare her fully to his gaze. She dragged her breasts down the remainder of his abdomen, then pressed them against his hard ridge before lifting to rid him of his slacks and boxers. But rather than returning to kiss his mouth, she straddled his leg. Sitting straight up, she cupped her breasts in her own hands, squeezing her nipples, knowing he was watching her raptly. Then she wantonly rubbed her wetness against the prickly hair covering his thigh, nearly causing herself to climax right on the spot.

He grasped her wrists and groaned. "Come here."

She stretched and grasped his hands, then drew his arms above his head.

"Shhh," she said, kissing him deeply as she rubbed her breasts against his chest again.

She curved his fingers around the wrought-iron

headboard, then slid back down again, running one of her nipples over his exposed length, then the other, before taking his turgid flesh in her hands. For long moments she visually examined the example of prime male virility, aware that his breathing was shallow and that he hadn't moved a muscle. She met his gaze as she licked the thick knob, then licked again to taste the bead of moisture there.

"Sweet Jesus…"

Drew threw back his head and gripped the headboard so tightly the entire bed shifted.

Josie went down on him, enjoying the salty taste, that he was watching her, that she knew exactly what to do to please a man as she fondled his soft, hair-covered sac.

When she sensed he was on the threshold of coming, she moved her other hand up and down the base of his shaft and increased the suction, thirsty for proof of his desire for her.

Instead, he growled and grasped her shoulders. She thought he was going to pull her away. But instead, he repositioned her so that she still had complete access to him…and he had the same access to her.

She carefully balanced her knees on either side of his head against his shoulders, then took him back into her mouth. When she felt his thumbs probe her engorged flesh, opening her to him, she nearly climaxed.

And moments later, when he fastened his mouth over her tight bud, she did come.

Drew marveled at the power he had over Josie as he breathed in her musk and absorbed her spasms and shudders. She not only smelled like fruit, she tasted and looked like it, too. He cupped her bottom, spreading the fleshy, split peach of her womanhood farther, drawing out her crisis by alternately suckling her then blowing on her, feeling her breasts crushing against his stomach and her fingers grip his thighs as she rode the wave of sensation.

When he was about to edge her bottom down toward his aching member, he felt her mouth take him in again. He was so unprepared for the move that his hips bucked involuntarily and he found himself coming with an intensity that made his balls ache.

For long, breathless moments he lay back, his mouth against her soft inner thigh. The room was dark but for the shaft of red light shining in from the club across the street. The ceiling fan whirled, blowing hot air against their moisture-covered bodies. He didn't know if he could continue their lovemaking. His climax had been so all consuming, he didn't think there was anything left for him to give.

Then he felt Josie shift slightly, lifting back up to her elbows. And that sweet mouth of hers was on him again.

He grasped her bottom and nudged her downward until she gripped his ankles and her swollen flesh was above his stiffening length. He reached for his slacks that were strewn across the bedside table and fished a condom out of his back pocket. Then he was parting the rounded globes of her perfect backside and thrusting upward, entering her in one, long, slick stroke to the hilt.

Josie let loose a moan that made his hard-on double in size. He thrust again, watching the latex glisten with her juices as his erection disappeared inside her, then reappeared again. He placed his thumbs on either side of her engorged labia, coaxing a deeper meeting as he thrust upward again. To his amazement, she found her own pleasure in her awkward position by grinding against him. The friction caused by her pubis against his balls made him grit his teeth to keep from coming again.

Slowly, she sat up so that she was straddling him reverse-cowgirl style. He stroked the long, graceful line of her back, then the swell of her bottom as she braced herself against his thighs and lifted herself off him, then dropped back down again. Then again.

He grasped her hips. "I want to watch you," he whispered harshly. "Turn around."

She did as asked, reaching down between them to reposition the tip of his arousal against her portal. Their gazes met as she slid down over him, inch by torturous inch, until he filled her to the hilt. She stretched out her long neck and moaned soulfully, rivaling the sound of the trumpet outside. Drew cupped her breasts as she moved, marveling in the way they filled his hands, the way they trembled with her movements. Then he splayed his hands against her slender hips, at first just letting them rest there as he watched her move against him, then guiding her movements, holding her still as he thrust hard up inside of her.

This enchantress was the most fascinating sight he'd ever seen. Her eyes fluttered open and she looked at him from under the fringe of her dark lashes. Up and down...up and down.

Yes, he thought, the word echoing in his mind. *Dear God, yes.*

This time when he came, he took her with him.

11

JOSIE FELT BLISSFULLY TIRED. After slipping from Drew's bed somewhere around dawn and going upstairs to her private rooms to take a shower, she went to the kitchen to put on some much needed coffee. She didn't see the need for an exercise routine because she got enough physical activity from taking care of the hotel. But her thighs and butt and even some aches in the backs of her arms were letting her know that perhaps she should look into at least doing some stretching.

Today was Monique's scheduled day off, and since Josie didn't know if Philippe would be feeling well enough to come in, she figured she'd better see to cleaning room 2B before officially opening the doors for the day. All the materials she'd need were in a supply closet on the second floor, so she climbed the back stairs from the kitchen, collected fresh linens and the bucket of cleaning supplies, and used her master key to open the door after a brief knock she knew wouldn't yield any results. Frederique never stayed the full night.

Josie pocketed the key and used her back to open the door. Normally, at night she would hear every creak and moan coming from this room, mostly because she was two floors upstairs in her room alone with nothing else to do. But last night, she and Drew had given Frederique and her guest a run for their money, at one point earning a quiet knock.

"Hey, keep it down over there. A body's trying to work," Frederique had said.

Josie turned to let the door close behind herself and took in the condition of the room. Only her gaze never made it beyond the bed. Because Frederique was draped over the end, face up, her throat cleanly slit from ear to ear. Just as Claire Laraway had been two weeks ago.

Josie dropped the linens and the cleaning bucket and smacked a rubber-gloved hand to her mouth, a sob welling up from the tips of her toes.

It looked like Frederique wasn't going to have to worry about working ever again.

DREW HAD BEEN DREAMING about Josie rubbing her breasts along the length of his rock-hard erection when a racket made him jackknife upright in bed. His gaze immediately swept the room. Josie was

gone. For a reason he couldn't explain, he felt like
something was wrong. He stripped back the sheet,
put on his slacks, then pulled open the door to his
room just in time to see Josie backing out of the
room next to his, her dark eyes wide and damp, her
mouth covered with a yellow-gloved hand.

"Josie?"

She jumped when he gently grasped her arms.

"Jesus, Josie, what's wrong?"

He maneuvered her to get a look inside the room
and that's when he saw exactly what was wrong.

He kicked the door so that it slammed against
the wall and then bounced shut.

"Come on."

Still barefoot and shirtless, he led a shell-
shocked Josie down the stairs to the lobby. She
seemed to regain her wits, taking the phone he'd
picked up and dialing 911.

"Detective Chevalier, please." A heartbeat of a
pause. "Find him…now."

JOSIE COULDN'T BELIEVE it had happened again. But
this time to someone she'd known.

Sitting at a wrought-iron table in the courtyard,
she couldn't seem to stop shivering, despite the
heat, aware that Drew stood nearby in the lobby
in case she should need him, while Detective

Chevalier loudly sipped coffee across from her. Police forensics teams were in and out of the place, trampling up the stairs and gathering evidence while she outlined the morning's events to Chevalier.

"This guest," he said, reviewing his notes. He looked even more rumpled than usual, his eyes bloodshot, his hair in need of a comb. Probably the department had woken him from a dead sleep— or a drunken stupor, by the looks of him. "Can you describe him?"

Josie shrugged, her own fingers wrapped so tightly around a cup of coffee she absently wondered if she'd ever be able to pry them free. "I told you, just like any other john."

He stared at her.

"Look, Detective—"

"Alan, please." He smiled at her. "I think we've known each other long enough now to move on to first names."

Josie didn't want to think of the reasons this man was in her life. Not when she couldn't seem to get the expression of horror on Frederique's face from her mind. "He looked like every other insurance salesman in town for a convention. Short. Paunchy. Balding. Glasses. With a couple of crisp, hundred-dollar bills to keep him happy."

"What's going on here?"

Josie looked up to find Philippe standing in the doorway to the courtyard.

"All right, Miss Villefranche. I suppose that's all for now." Chevalier sat back in his chair. "Send Mr. Morrison in on your way to the lobby."

Josie grabbed Philippe's arm on the way out, telling him a shorthand version of how she'd found Frederique that morning.

"Holy mother of God. What's going on in this place?" he said quietly as they both watched Drew walk into the courtyard and take the seat opposite the detective.

"The voodoo's got you but good."

Josie swung around to find Anne-Marie in the middle of the lobby as if she had been there for some time, absorbing the atmosphere.

"Ma'am, I'm afraid you have to stay on the other side of the yellow tape," a uniformed police officer said.

Anne-Marie stared at him. "You can't keep the bad out with that flimsy piece of tape, Officer."

The young man rolled his eyes and escorted her nearer Josie and Philippe.

The lobby had been split right down the middle with crime-scene tape, barring anyone access from upstairs or the front desk. Not that it mattered. Josie didn't think she'd be seeing any business today. Or any other day in the near future for that matter.

She suddenly felt dizzy.

"Whoa." Philippe grasped her arm. "Are you okay?"

"Fine…I'm fine." At least she was doing worlds better than Frederique and Claire Laraway were doing. "I just haven't had much to eat since yesterday morning, that's all."

"Let's go to the kitchen." Philippe threw a glance at the officer standing with his arms crossed over his chest. "Unless they have that cordoned off, too."

The officer swept his arm toward the back of the hotel but stopped short of saying, "Be my guest."

Philippe led the way through the courtyard with Josie on his heels. Anne-Marie slowed her steps as they neared the detective and Drew. Josie grabbed her arm and towed her into the kitchen.

Her friend's bracelets jangled. "There's something not right about that man," she said. "But I can't seem to get a clear handle on what, exactly, it is."

"You think he might have killed Frederique?" Philippe asked.

Josie sat on one of the stools, smoothing her hands unconsciously against the cutting board. "Don't be ridiculous."

"Why would it be ridiculous?" Philippe asked,

getting three extra-large mugs from a cupboard and going about making café au lait.

"Because he was nowhere near New Orleans when Claire Laraway was killed."

"That doesn't mean he couldn't have killed Frederique."

Anne-Marie had stayed silent during the exchange, her gaze on Josie's face.

"Mr. Morrison couldn't have done it," she said quietly. "Mr. Morrison was otherwise occupied last night."

Philippe gaped at Josie. "You didn't."

"I did."

If she should have been surprised at how easily the admission of her relationship with Drew came, she wasn't. She'd known what she was getting into: a temporary connection based solely on sex.

She shivered, thinking about just how very good that sex was.

"What do you know about him?" Philippe asked.

Josie regarded him from under lowered brows. "Aside from he's hot and great in bed?"

He placed the three full bowl-like mugs on the cutting board and pulled up the stool next to hers. "You can start there. Is he as good as I think he is?"

The Harlequin Reader Service® — Here's how it works:

Accepting your 2 free books and mystery gift places you under no obligation to buy anything. You may keep the books and gift and return the shipping statement marked "cancel." If you do not cancel, about a month later we'll send you 6 additional books and bill you just $3.99 each in the U.S., or $4.47 each in Canada, plus 25¢ shipping & handling per book and applicable taxes if any.* That's the complete price and — compared to cover prices of $4.75 each in the U.S., and $5.75 each in Canada – it's quite a bargain! You may cancel at any time, but if you choose to continue, every month we'll send you 6 more books which you may either purchase at the discount price or return to us and cancel your subscription.

*Terms and prices subject to change without notice. Sales tax applicable in N.Y. Canadian residents will be charged applicable provincial taxes and GST.

Anne-Marie chose to remain standing. "Josie let him in her bed. That says enough."

Actually, she hadn't let him into her bed, per se. But she knew what her friend was saying.

Philippe gave a dramatic eye roll. "I want details."

"He's a car-parts salesman in town for a convention," she said, dipping melba toast into her café au lait and biting down.

Philippe objected. "That's not what I meant."

"I know."

"He doesn't look like any car-parts salesman I've ever seen," Anne-Marie said with a shake of her head, her bracelets jangling as she sipped out of her own mug and reached for a piece of melba toast from the package in front of Josie.

If the thought mirrored Josie's own thought when she'd first met Drew, she wasn't saying.

"Look," she said after swallowing. "He's just like every other guy who comes through the city on business looking for a little fun."

The fact that she'd said the same words about Frederique's "date" last night didn't escape her notice.

"Just a hell of a lot sexier."

"Killers can be sexy," Philippe pointed out.

"Do you want another innocent man arrested in

connection with this hotel? Isn't it bad enough that Claude Lafitte was wrongly accused of killing Claire Laraway?"

Josie suddenly lost her appetite.

She put down the rest of the toast and wiped her hands absently on a paper napkin.

"Josie?" Philippe prompted, making her realize she'd lost track of the conversation.

She slid from the stool. "I need to get back to work."

Of course it would have been nice if she actually had work to get back to.

DREW LET HIMSELF into the hotel room. Only it wasn't at the Josephine; it was at the Marriott on the other side of the Quarter. The hotel hosting the convention he claimed to be attending.

His change in residence had nothing to do with his possibly being under suspicion for the murder of Frederique. No. He had work to do and that was virtually impossible at Josie's. Aside from not having access to his room there after being escorted to collect his briefcase, the Josephine didn't have the modern conveniences of this hotel. Namely Internet access and air-conditioning.

It also didn't have Josie.

He placed his briefcase on top of the bed, took

out his laptop, then set it up on the desk in the corner. He flicked on a light, then went to stand at the window. The Marriott was worlds away from Josie's place in the Old French Quarter, even though it was within walking distance. From up here, the short buildings and houses that made up the Quarter didn't look quaint or even real. Instead they appeared crowded together and in need of repair, roofs slanting, wrought-iron railings chipped and broken in spots. In the light of day, the area looked like an old painted lady whose time had long passed, her lipstick cracked and out of place on her wrinkled face.

He ran his hand over his own face.

The homicide detective who had interviewed him had made no secret of his suspicions that Drew was involved in the murder of Frederique. Since he'd been the only other guest in residence, it was natural, he supposed. But should the detective start scratching beyond the surface of Drew's story, his entire cover would be blown.

Suddenly filling his mind was an image of Josie's beautiful face smiling down at him as she straddled his hips, her honey-colored skin glistening, her limber body spent.

How would she look at him when she discovered who he really was and what he was there for?

Muttering a string of profanities, he stepped to the desk and pulled out the chair. Moments later, his computer was booted and he was doing research on the area immediately around Josie's hotel. He picked up the phone to call his client.

"Christ, Morrison, we want her out. We don't want the place so damaged we can't do anything with it."

"Are you implying I had something to do with last night's events?" he asked, sitting back in the chair as if pushed against it.

"Let's just say that we're familiar with your reputation."

Drew fell silent. Sure, he was known to be ruthless, but not to the extent his client was implying. Did they really think he was capable of murder in order to force a target into selling?

"I'm a closer, not a killer," he said evenly.

"Then close this damn thing."

The client hung up on him.

Drew snapped his cell phone shut then sat staring at it.

Is that how he was really viewed in the professional community? As a white-collar hit man of sorts? The one they called in when someone needed to get his hands dirty, and they wanted to make sure not a speck of mud could be found on their person?

He realized with a fist to the gut that that's exactly how he was viewed. And a month ago— hell, only a few days ago—he would have taken the comment as a compliment. Isn't that what he'd spent the past ten years of his life doing? Building himself up as the kind of man who got things done, no matter what it took?

He gained access to the Internet and began typing in search strings.

It was time to redefine himself. Not only in his own eyes. But also in the eyes of those he worked with.

12

MUCH LATER THAT NIGHT, long after the police had finally left and Philippe had helped her clean up the mess they had made Josie sat at the front desk, going over the events. The front doors were open, the shotgun under the desk within easy reach. The back door was double locked.

She'd insisted Philippe go home. She didn't want to risk his having a relapse. She needed him here as much as possible in the coming days. She'd be able to hold her own for the night.

At least that's what she'd thought when she'd assumed Drew would be returning. But she hadn't heard a word from him all day. Not since he'd left after talking to Detective Chevalier.

"Stay away from that guy, Jos," Philippe had told her before leaving. "If I didn't know you'd kick me out, I'd insist on staying tonight just to keep you two apart."

"He doesn't have anything to do with what's

going on," she'd insisted. "You'll see that he doesn't."

But now that the hours were stretching, and he hadn't bothered contacting her, she was beginning to think Philippe and Anne-Marie might be right.

Of course, the alternative was that he was done with her. He'd had his fun and was ready to move on.

What did it say about her that she preferred to think of him as somehow involved in the shady go-ings-on around the Josephine?

Given that there were now two murders that appeared linked together, both rooms 2D and 2B were blocked off, yellow crime-scene tape ban-ning entrance. Not only couldn't she enter them, she couldn't scrub the room in which Frederique had been murdered, which bothered her to no end thinking that her blood still stained the mattress and the floor.

"You're damn lucky I don't just shut the whole operation down," Detective Chevalier had told her. "The whole freakin' hotel is a crime scene."

The phone rang near her elbow. Josie jumped, not realizing how wired she was until that mo-ment.

She snatched it up in the middle of the second ring, her heart beating wildly in her chest.

"Drew?"

She hadn't realized that's what she was going to say until the name was out of her mouth.

"Josie?"

A female voice.

She closed her eyes and forced a deep breath. Not just any female voice, but that of her cousin.

"Look, I heard what went down there today," Sabine said. "Are you all right?"

It was difficult to believe in light of all that had gone on in the past year that she and Sabine had once been very close. Much more like sisters than cousins. She remembered times when they'd dressed up in white gloves and sat with their dolls, drinking tea in the courtyard, feeling a part of the adult world.

Josie looked at the dark and empty courtyard now, wishing for those times again.

"Yes, I'm fine. Thanks for asking." And she meant it.

"So, does that mean you're finally ready to give this hotel sale a shot?"

Josie's breath was stolen straight from her.

She slowly took the telephone away from her ear, her fist gripping it tightly, and hung up. She had no more words to say to Sabine. They'd been over this so many times Josie couldn't count.

When *Granme* had died, leaving everything to Josie—which was the Josephine and all her many problems—Sabine and her mother had balked, laying claim to half of Josie's inheritance. They'd tried to obtain legal counsel to sue her for half, only they couldn't come up with an attorney willing to take the case because Sabine and her mother had a long history of staged accidents and welfare fraud.

Until five months ago. Josie had been visited by a corpulent attorney in a white linen suit and straw hat hired by Sabine and her mother to threaten her with a lawsuit.

Josie had tried to make right from the beginning. She, as well, had been surprised *Granme* had left her the hotel and everything in it, giving her daughters and other living grandchild, Sabine, only pictures and mementos. Of course, her own mother had yet to surface to claim her sentimental inheritance. It still sat in a pink box in the corner of Josie's closet upstairs just in case she did show.

She'd been brainstorming ways to work everything out in a way that wouldn't involve selling the Josephine when her cousin had started calling, threatening to take the entire hotel away from her. Between trying to hang on to the hotel and being on the defensive, she'd never really had a chance to come up with something that might work for all of them.

And at this point, she didn't have it in her to care anymore. If Sabine was going to sue, she was going to sue. Only, Josie had never heard from that attorney again…

She stared at the phone. Could Sabine be behind the late-night phone calls she'd been receiving? How about the voodoo ritual she'd found in room 2D the other night? She wouldn't put it past her cousin.

While *Granme* had always raised her to believe she had no one to take care of her but herself and that she should do so with integrity and pride, her cousin seemed to believe everyone owed her something. Government? *Give me money, I deserve it.* A woman with a nice car who made the mistake of going to the wrong supermarket? *You backed into me, no matter that I made sure you would. Pay up.*

Josie didn't think her cousin had ever worked an honest day in her life. And when she'd offered Sabine a job at the hotel, her cousin had laughed at her, apparently above toiling away at a menial job, no matter the pay. Of course, she'd also said that if she took a job that was on the books, she'd lose her government checks. The same applied when Josie had offered to put Sabine's name on the hotel's deed. She'd lose her government benefits. Couldn't Josie just sell the hotel and give her the money, real hush-hush like, so welfare wouldn't find out about it?

She pushed up from the chair and walked toward the door. Outside on the street, the world continued to turn, people continued to live, and nothing stopped for anyone. She didn't realize that she held the latest offer from the hotel chain that was aggressively pursuing her to sell the Josephine, until she was staring at it. She swallowed hard. She'd never once seriously considered the offer.

Until right at that moment.

After the first couple offers, she'd stopped opening the envelopes, merely stuck them in a drawer under the front desk. Now she ripped open the end and shook out the letter within, then unfolded the single piece of thick stock paper. The amount they were offering had gone up significantly. It was surely enough to cover her debts, give Sabine the money she was looking for and see to it Josie got a fresh start.

Fresh start where?

She looked over her shoulder at the lobby. She didn't know anything else but the Josephine. What else could she do?

She held the letter tightly. Selling would mean

no more sleepless nights. No more eighteen-hour days spent doing nothing for stretches at a time. No more dealing with leering old men who insisted on thinking the right dollar amount would put her in their beds for the night.

No more fearing that a killer somewhere out there in the sea of faces had her name on his list.

A loud thud coming from the lobby behind her sent her pulse racing. Whipping around, she searched the shadows to no avail. She looked back over her shoulder at the crowded street filled with people who didn't have a clue of the fear she felt, much less could care. She reached to shut the doors, then thought better of it. She didn't want to close herself in should she have company.

Her pulse pounding in her ears, she crept slowly forward, her ears alert, her eyes wide. All the lights were off except for the dim emergency lights leading up the stairs and a small pool of light created by the banker's lamp on the front desk where she'd been sitting. The farther away she moved from the door, the louder her heartbeat sounded. The more isolated she felt.

The lobby smelled of candle wax and furniture polish. The tall plants cast eerie shadows against the walls. Too many dark places for someone to hide. No one around to care.

That thought more than anything caused Josie's chest to hurt.

No matter the warnings or how well *Granme* had tried to prepare her, there was no way she could have been ready for the sheer loneliness that would descend on her upon her grandmother's death. She had no one. Not a single person she could turn to with her fears or for help.

No Drew...

She hadn't realized how profoundly his absence was affecting her until that moment.

She'd taken her sandals off earlier and now her bare feet padded over the grit dusting the marble tile, the shells around her ankle quietly clinking together.

She was almost to the desk and the light there. More importantly, the shotgun she had hidden behind it was nearly within reach. She might not have anyone, but she had herself. She'd done a pretty good job of taking care of herself for the past year, and for some time before that when *Granme* had given her more responsibility at the hotel. She'd do the same now.

With a shaking hand, she reached over the desk and lifted the weapon with a minimum of noise. She tucked the butt between her arm and rib cage and pulled the cocking mechanism, metal scratching against metal as buckshot shells were loaded into the gun, ready to be fired through the short barrel.

Fear no longer paralyzing her, she gave the lobby another quick scan, noticing a broom she had propped against the wall behind the desk had fallen over.

She dropped the gun to her side.

"You're letting all this voodoo crap get to you," she muttered to herself.

A loud shriek sounded at the same time as something launched in her direction. Quick thinking kept her from filling the black cat with buckshot.

Josie was convinced her heart hadn't just leaped into her throat; it had catapulted from her body altogether.

"Jesus, Jez, what in the hell's gotten into you?"

The cat wound around and around her legs, rubbing the side of her face against Josie's ankle.

"Oh, sweetie, I'm sorry," she said, putting the shotgun back behind the desk and scooping the old feline up into her arms. "I forgot to put food out for you today, didn't I?"

Jezebel's response was a loud purr as she licked Josie's chin.

Scratching the cat behind the ears, she headed toward the kitchen.

She pushed open the door and Jez jumped from her arms, scratching her arm in the process.

"Ow." Josie switched on the overhead light and checked the shallow scratch. Thankfully there was no blood, but it wouldn't hurt to put some disinfectant on it.

She wondered how the cat had managed to get in.

A loud meow and a hiss drew her attention toward the back of the kitchen. The door she had locked and double locked an hour ago stood wide open, the screen door squeaking on its hinges.

And Josie was without her shotgun.

13

JOSIE COULDN'T BELIEVE that someone had gained access to the back door…again.

She positioned a two-by-four diagonally across the closed doorway and took a nail out of her mouth, then hammered it in. She repeated the process with twenty nails until she was convinced that there was no way anyone was going to be coming through that door again until she could get the locks changed.

She looked over her shoulder at the brightly lit kitchen. She only hoped she had locked the intruder out instead of in.

After picking up the shotgun from the cutting-board table, Josie made her way back out through the courtyard and into the lobby, Jez following on her heels. She'd switched on all the lights so not a shadow remained, and had even gone through the rooms upstairs, although she was relatively certain whoever had gained access to the kitchen hadn't made it up the stairs. She would have heard them.

She glanced down at the inexplicably friendly feline. "Have you decided to keep me company tonight?"

Jez rubbed Josie's shin with her nose.

Josie picked her up with her free hand. "Good. I could use some."

She'd already locked the front door and put a Closed sign in the window. While it wasn't the first time she'd been alone in the hotel, that way, it was certainly the first time she was overly aware of it.

And if Drew returned?

For some reason she couldn't explain, she knew he wouldn't be coming back tonight.

And maybe not for any other night.

The possibility made her feel even lonelier.

DREW SAT BACK FROM where he'd been diligently working at the desk and glanced at his watch. After midnight.

Shit.

He'd been so engrossed with the information he was uncovering on his client, that he hadn't realized how late it had gotten.

Josie...

His throat tightened. He was surprised that the

first person who entered his mind was her. Then again, maybe it wasn't so much surprise as a realization.

What he was coming to understand was that his connection to the exotic hotel owner involved more than just fantastic sex.

He got up from the chair, checking to make sure he had his wallet, cell phone and card key before leaving the room. He took the elevator to the lobby then stepped outside. He envisioned her sitting at the front desk of Hotel Josephine, cooling herself with that lacy fan he'd seen her use the first time he'd laid eyes on her.

Days had passed, but rather than the city giving itself over to autumn, it appeared to be getting hotter still. He didn't know if that was the norm, but he did know that he was getting used to the heat, his body adjusting so that he didn't find walks like the one he was taking now as taxing as he would have a few days ago.

Instead, what the heat did to him, especially since he'd just spent the day in an air-conditioned room, was make his body remember all the hot things he and Josie had done last night. He glanced down to make sure that his arousal—brought on by merely thinking about her dark, lush body— wasn't having an obvious effect. While more unusual things had probably been seen on Bourbon Street, he was no exhibitionist.

This was a first for him, this incessant lust he felt for Josie Villefranche. He couldn't seem to get enough of her, no matter how much sex they had or how often he was in her presence. In the year that had passed since his divorce, his social life had included a few select women, none of them making it far beyond the morning after. Hell, even with Carol, his ex, he couldn't remember feeling this way. Perhaps he had, back in the beginning of their relationship, but what had transpired between then and now had sullied all that, making what he was feeling for Josie fresh and new and perplexing.

Never, ever had he turned his professional attentions toward helping a mark before.

He slid his right hand into his pocket, pondering that reality.

He was hired to do a job and he did it. That's where his interest began and ended. Only this was no longer just a job to him. Not this one. Not Josie. So he'd begun digging. And he wasn't so much surprised by what he'd uncovered as he was enlightened.

It seemed Rove had bought the two buildings to the right of Josie's establishment, the private residence to the left, and also held the deeds to a warehouse behind the Josephine.

Obviously Dick Rove's intention had never been to renovate the hotel and make a go of it. He planned to raze it and build a bigger hotel, something more befitting the Royal Emperor Suites family of hotels.

If Drew hadn't been so distracted by how small-time the job had been and so focused on the next job he wanted to win, he'd probably have picked up on that.

Then he'd let Josie into his life.

Or, rather, she'd sneaked into his mind and heart like a bewitching enchantress.

So Rove had a lot more riding on the outcome of this project than Drew had originally suspected. Which led him back to his earlier suspicion that Rove also had someone else working the case.

But who? And was he or she responsible for what was happening?

Drew neared the hotel, taking in the old place and her flower-decorated balconies and dark windows. Was the building on the city's historical register? If it wasn't, then Josie should take measures to make sure it was placed there immediately. Also, he needed to check into the laws that would prevent Rove from building something not in line with the architectural integrity of the area. Laws Drew's client may have already bypassed by greasing a few of the right palms.

The Mississippi River wasn't the only thing that ran crooked down here.

Drew stopped in front of the double doors. Closed. He cupped a hand and looked inside. Dark.

Damn.

Had Josie closed up and gone to bed?

He rang the bell he knew would alert her up in her private rooms.

Nothing.

He stepped back and looked up at the fourth floor. He thought he saw movement near the balcony to what he guessed was her room, but he couldn't be sure.

What he could be sure of was that she wasn't going to answer the door. And he realized it was no more than he deserved after deserting her.

He waited for five minutes, then wove his way through the tourists back toward the Marriott.

JUST AFTER DAWN, Josie locked the hotel after herself, leaving a note for Monique and Philippe that they should take the day off and that she'd call them later. She tucked her handbag under her arm and watched as Jez scampered down the street, surprisingly limber given her age. Apparently she was satisfied that her company was no longer needed and was off to do whatever it was she did between feeding times.

Josie glanced around the street before choosing a direction. At this time of the morning, the area looked like a ghost town. Stores and clubs and restaurants were closed up tight, discarded cups and litter dotted the curbs and sidewalks, and the stench of urine and beer was strong. At somewhere around ten, when everyone stirred to start the workday over again, employees would sweep and water down the sidewalks and street in front of their places of business. Until then, it looked like someone had held a party and left a helluva mess.

Josie was used to it. This was where she'd grown up. She knew which corners the homeless preferred for sleeping. Knew which puddles not to walk through. Which alleys to steer clear of.

Of course, trying to focus on her surroundings was a diversionary tactic that wasn't quite working. She'd gotten little sleep last night. Not just because of her mysterious back-door visitor. But also because all she could see was Drew's somber face as he'd stood on the street below, waiting for her to open the door.

For some reason she couldn't define, she'd simply peered through the balcony doors at him, leaving him standing there. Perhaps it was an instinctual reaction designed for self-protection. Not from physical harm. But from emotional devastation.

She'd never have expected that she would come to feel what she was for the striking, grinning stranger from Kansas City. She'd had great sex before without attaching herself to the individual. But with Drew...

With Drew, all she had to do was think his name and her pulse thickened and her heart gave an off beat.

If pressed to point at any one reason for her uncharacteristic behavior, she couldn't have done it. It was the way he put his hands on her and the way he didn't. It was what he whispered into her ear and what he left unsaid. It was the way he slept with his arm protectively encircling her, as if he didn't want to let her go. It was the way he did release her without her saying a word, seeming to understand her need for freedom and independence.

It was everything. It was nothing.

And she had as much control over it as she did her own heartbeat.

A trombone player was already setting up on a

corner, using his case as a chair while he polished his instrument, a small cigar box at his feet for change. He spotted Josie and smiled.

"Morning, Miss Villefranche."

"Good morning, Harry. How's life treating you?" She tossed a dollar bill into his box.

"Better all the time."

She smiled and continued down the street.

It took her about twenty minutes to walk to her destination. Thankfully the caretaker had already opened the gates, which were closed at night because the voodoo queen Marie Laveau's grave had been looted one too many times by tourists and locals alike. She passed the aboveground tomb in question, which was decorated with all sorts of mementos and voodoo icons, walking silently between the narrow rows until she reached the far wall. She paused for a long moment, unmoving, then touched the plaque engraved with her grandmother's name.

In the past year, it seemed only this place was able to give Josie a sense of peace she'd lost along with Josephine Villefranche. Her mind cleared of all thought and her body relaxed, the act of being there giving her a sense of life's cycles. Her, her mother, her grandmother and her mother before her. Each woman different yet with the same blood running through their veins.

Even her cousin figured in there, as part of a long line of strong Villefranche females.

"*Granme*, I need your help," she said quietly, the raised lettering defined under her fingertips. "I've fallen in love."

She hadn't been aware that's what she was going to say when she'd opened her mouth, but there it was. Two women had been murdered at the Josephine, and she was in danger of losing the hotel altogether, but it was her conflicted emotions for Drew Morrison that had drawn her here, searching for some of her grandmother's no-nonsense advice.

Although, she understood that even her grandmother hadn't always been the wise woman she remembered. Josie's mother and aunt stood as clear reminders of that. When Josephine Villefranche had been younger than Josie was now, she'd fallen for a man. A brush salesman traveling through town. A handsome white man whose name Josie had never learned, although he had been her grandfather.

"Beware of love, Josie." She heard *Granme's* voice as clearly as if she'd been standing right beside her. "Love is the one thing over which you have no control. It can make you stronger or it can destroy you."

Josie had been all of ten at the time and had

knocked on her grandmother's door during one of her "spells," short periods of time when she'd withdraw from hotel duties and stay in her rooms, shut off from the world.

"Which did it make you, *Granme?*" she'd asked, settling into an armchair across from where her grandmother sat staring toward the windows. Windows that had been covered by sheers, blurring the scene beyond.

"Both."

Josie opened her eyes and stared at the plaque.

If you didn't have a choice in who or how you loved, did you then not have a choice in how that love affected you? Could you decide whether it made you stronger or destroyed you?

And therein lay the danger she suspected her grandmother had been trying to make her aware of.

Here she was with problems piled on her doorstep, and rather than seeking ways to save a hotel that was as much a part of her heritage as her grandmother had been, she was instead searching for answers to questions that had no practical relevance.

"Men are the devil, Josie. Especially white men. They mean no harm. They saunter in with their natty clothes and charming grins and make you feel like the most beautiful woman on earth.

But then they'll leave you behind like a bag of garbage at the curb."

"How are white men different from black men, *Granme?*"

She'd pointed a gnarled finger at Josie. "Because you expect the black men to stay."

So had her grandmother expected, or at least hoped, that her white lover would stay and marry her? Had he even known their brief affair had produced a child?

And had Josie's mother decided not to make the same mistakes her own mother before her had? Had she seen her chance to get that forever and sacrificed everything in order to get it?

Were there days she regretted her decision? Or was she even now completely happy and content?

Josie dropped her hand from the plaque.

"This place, this hotel, it will never betray you, girl. It will never take up with another woman, or leave you pregnant, or move on to the next town without you. Remember that. Respect that."

Josie opened her purse and fished inside for a silver dollar, which she placed on a small shelf below the plaque. She left her fingers on top, pondering the many words her grandmother had imparted. The advice, the warnings, the wisdom.

Never had she considered the possibility that much of it was born of a woman scorned.

She squared her shoulders. "I'm going to save the hotel, *Granme*. Of that you can be sure."

Then she turned and made her way back through the graveyard, a new resolve filling her.

14

DREW KNEW ONE THING and one thing only: he had to come clean with Josie. Tell her exactly who he was and what he had come there to do…and what he now wanted to do. Or, rather, wanted to help *her* to do. And that was to save her hotel.

At around nine-thirty the next morning, after having made calls to check the liquidity of his cash resources, he headed to the hotel, only to find a note on the door meant for Josie's employees. He read it, then returned it to where it had been.

Where was she? While he would be the last to profess to know Josie better than anyone else, he sensed that she wasn't the type of person just to up and leave her hotel with the Closed sign hanging in the window if there wasn't a good reason.

Was she inside?

He rang the bell then stepped back to look up at the doors to her rooms. In fact, the doors to all the rooms were closed. It was the first time he'd seen that.

He knew a moment of concern. Then another thought quickly followed: had she given up and was even now arranging to sell the hotel to Dick Rove?

He dialed his client, his back teeth clenched tightly together at the thought of Rove taking the hotel from her.

Rove's secretary told him he was unavailable but offered to take a message. Drew didn't leave one. Instead he slapped his cell phone closed and looked around the street. He wouldn't know where to begin looking for her. He just hoped she wasn't with the other "closer" Rove had hired to work Josie.

A person Drew suspected might be setting him up to take a fall, as well.

Damn.

A bar across the street had just opened its doors and a young man wearing an apron was spraying down the sidewalk and curb.

Drew held out a twenty-dollar bill. "Have any coffee in there?"

The kid smiled. "No, but I will."

Drew took a seat right near the door with a clear view of the front of the hotel. He had no choice but to wait.

"WHERE IN THE HELL have you been? I've been waiting here for over an hour."

Josie considered Philippe where he'd appeared next to her. It was just after two in the afternoon and it had been a long day for her so far.

She unlocked the front door and took the note and the Closed sign off before leading the way into the lobby.

"Seeing to a few things," she said noncommittally.

"I've been worried sick. What do you mean by closing the place like that? You could have waited until I came in to do whatever business you needed to do."

She wanted to reassure him, but she was so physically and mentally weary that she merely spared him a look as she put her purse away under the desk.

"What was so urgent that you needed to see to it so early, anyway?"

"Business matters."

"What business matters?"

Josie stared at him for a moment. Philippe had never taken that much interest in the business aside from wanting to know when he'd get paid.

He ran a hand through his already tousled hair. "Sorry. I guess I'm just all worked up."

She shuffled through some papers.

"I was worried about you."

She smiled at him.

He smiled back. "Why don't I go fix us a bite to eat and we'll have a chat."

Josie tucked the papers under her arm. "Can't. I have some things to do." She started toward the stairs. "And you don't have the time, either. Open up the balcony doors to air out the rooms and see to the front desk until I come back down."

"Josie?"

It wasn't Philippe who'd said her name. Rather, someone who'd just entered the lobby had. And he wasn't alone.

Claude Lafitte and FBI agent Akela Brooks.

It wasn't all that long ago that Claude had been a regular at the Josephine. Then he'd been accused of the murder of Claire Laraway and had then taken Akela hostage at gunpoint.

That had been almost three weeks ago and all had turned out well so far as Josie could tell. The newspaper had been filled with the news that a romance had developed between the former captor and captive. A definite case of opposites attract, given Claude's deep bayou roots and Akela's high-society family background.

"We heard about the second murder," Akela said, not bothering with niceties. Something for which Josie was thankful because she wasn't in a nice mood.

Claude cursed. "More like we were paid a visit by Chevalier to check up on my whereabouts on the night in question."

She eyed Claude for a long moment. The first murder had never been solved, and since Claude had been with the victim the night before she'd been killed, he'd been the police's first—and apparently only—suspect.

She still wasn't straight on all the details, but Claude had been cleared.

The telephone on the front desk rang and Philippe picked it up.

"Josie, it's for you."

She was about to take it when Akela asked, "Do you have a few minutes?" Her demeanor was calm and cool, but her eyes held shadows of worry.

Josie regarded her, then looked toward the front desk. "Take a message, Philippe. And can you fix some coffee for the three of us?"

DREW STOPPED PACING the length of his hotel room and slowly closed his cell phone. At least he'd finally gotten an answer.

This morning, he'd sat at that bar for over three hours waiting for Josie to return. He'd finally given up and had returned to the Marriott where he'd called the Josephine every ten minutes or so. He eyed the papers strewn across the king-size bed. But why wouldn't she take the call? Since Philippe had asked for a message—that Drew hadn't left—he assumed the guy hadn't known who Drew was, so he had no reason to believe she just didn't want to talk to *him*.

He hated that he hadn't been able to speak with her but he did feel better knowing she was back at the hotel.

Gathering up the documents, he put them in order then dropped them into his briefcase before snapping it closed.

Since he knew she was at the hotel, then he could go see her.

Josie sat by herself in the courtyard long after Claude and Akela had left with promises to check back later and see how Josie was doing.

Claude had been released from custody and all charges against him dropped. Physical evidence had been found that didn't belong to him or the victim, namely a hair inside the neck wound itself, as if purposely placed there.

Why hadn't she been told about this evidence?

She pressed her fingertips to her temples, trying to recall seeing anyone else on that fateful morning.

Then there was the fact that the police suspected Frederique's murder had been a copycat killing. It had been determined that she had been brutally raped before being killed, a detail not in line with the first murder.

Philippe took the empty chair opposite Josie.

"You ready to tell me what's going on?"

She blinked at him, taking a moment to attach his words to their meaning.

Seeing him made her recall what she had been about to do before her visitors had arrived. She got to her feet, gathering up the papers on the table in front of her.

"Nothing's going on, Philippe," she said quietly, her mind already on the tasks she needed to see to. "At least nothing I can share right now."

He got up, as well. "Then that means there *is* something going on."

She started toward the lobby, heading for the stairs beyond, and was startled when Philippe grasped her arm.

She stared at him.

"Come on, Josie, don't you think I deserve to know what's going on? I mean, my job's on the line here."

"Don't worry. I'll let you know the minute I think it's something you should know."

She couldn't really explain why, but he was beginning to irritate her. She looked down at where he still held her arm.

"Everything all right, Miss Villefranche?"

Josie glanced at Detective Chevalier standing in the garden doorway wearing his requisite wrinkled overcoat and holding his hat. While he'd spoken to her, his gaze was very obviously on Philippe.

Philippe released her abruptly, looking abashed. "I'm sorry. I'm just really worked up about everything going on here lately," he said quietly.

Josie smiled at him softly. "I know. I am, too." She glanced at the detective. "Everything's fine."

Philippe disappeared into the kitchen and she turned to face Chevalier, crossing her arms over her chest. "What can I do for you, Detective?"

He fiddled with the brim of his hat, turning it in a circle. "Could you have Mr. Morrison come down, please?"

Josie straightened the papers she still held in her hands. "Mr. Morrison isn't here."

"Do you know where I might find him?"

"At the convention is my guess." She brushed past him on her way toward the front desk.

"Ah, that's right. He's in town on business, isn't he?"

There was a touch of unmistakable irony to his voice that caught Josie's attention. "Has there been any progress on solving either of the murders that occurred in my establishment, Detective?"

He squinted at her. "I don't know. It all depends."

"Depends on what?"

"On what Mr. Morrison has to say."

She leaned against the front desk. "I've already told you, he was with me the night of the murder."

"Yes, but you also told me he was in town for a convention."

"You just said yourself he was here for business."

"Yes, but apparently an auto-parts convention doesn't factor into that business. It's my guess that Mr. Morrison wouldn't know a gasket from an air filter."

Josie didn't like where this was heading. Her skin felt suddenly cold. "I don't know what you mean."

"I'm sure you don't."

She carefully placed her papers on the desk. Getting anything from Chevalier was like pulling teeth and up until now she hadn't made the effort. Although, given the information Claude and Akela had shared, maybe she should have.

"Are you going to tell me what's going on, Detective?" she asked, crossing her arms again so tightly that she cut off circulation. "Or are we going to play more word games?"

He stepped to the other side of the desk and put his hat down. "How well do you know Mr. Morrison?"

Josie felt her cheeks flush. She'd already answered that question and didn't care to have to repeat herself.

"Oh, wait." He took his notepad out of his overcoat pocket and thumbed through its battered item. "You and he are engaged in a sexual relationship. Temporary."

She glanced toward the courtyard, unable to meet his gaze. She'd been the one to add the word *temporary*. Because at the time, that's what she'd believed it to be. The problem was she was coming to see that there wasn't anything temporary about her growing feelings for Drew.

"That's right."

"So is it over?"

She recalled Drew standing outside on the street late last night and her chest gave a none-too-subtle squeeze. "Seeing as Mr. Morrison has checked out, I'd chance a yes."

Chevalier smiled as he put his notepad back into his pocket.

"Oh, I have it on good authority that he'll be back," he said, placing his hat on his head.

Her heart gave a hopeful lilt even as dread spread in her stomach. "How can you be so sure?"

"Because he hasn't done what he came here to accomplish yet."

She didn't say anything as he walked toward the door.

He turned before stepping outside. "He hasn't gotten you to sell the hotel."

15

HE WAS TOO LATE.

Drew knew that the moment he entered the hotel and the assistant manager, Philippe, considered him with barely concealed contempt.

He'd had a bad inkling all morning. Actually, since last night he'd had the strange suspicion that somehow, some way, Josie had learned the truth about him. And that had bothered him beyond his capacity to deal with it just then.

He looked around the lobby and courtyard and didn't spot the person he was looking for, the only one who mattered in this entire situation.

"Where's Josie?"

Philippe crossed his arms. "Wouldn't you like to know?"

"That's why I asked."

"She doesn't want to see you."

There it was. What Drew had been dreading: she knew.

He turned toward the stairs.

Philippe moved faster than Drew would have thought possible, blocking his progress. "Whoa. Where do you think you're going?"

"To find her."

"I told you she doesn't want to see you."

Drew stared down the younger man, suppressing the urge to remove him physically from his path. He was surprised by the primal desire. For the past decade he'd used words to make his point, to wage his business war. He hadn't resorted to physical confrontation since his stint in the military.

It didn't help that his adversary seemed to be egging him on, as if he wanted Drew to take a swing at him. Which gave him considerable cause for pause.

"That's all right, Philippe."

They both turned to see Josie standing at the top of the stairs.

For an all too brief moment, the world stopped turning. Or rather, it began revolving again, propelling life in the right direction.

Drew's breath froze in his lungs. While Josie was wearing a summery dress similar to the others he'd seen her in, she could have been wearing a slinky evening gown, the way the sight of her stopped his heart. Just looking at her made him feel not himself somehow. As if the moment she entered a room, a part of him fused with her, as if they were two parts of one whole instead of separate entities.

The sensation was unfamiliar to him. And left him feeling unprotected. As if he were in the middle of a clearing with twenty sniper rifles aimed at him.

The expression on her face told him she was experiencing some similar emotions that she didn't quite know how to handle either.

Her expression also told him that he'd lost something he'd never be able to regain: her trust.

"Can I talk to you?" he asked.

Philippe spoke, "Haven't you already said and done enough?"

Josie started down the stairs. "I'll be in the kitchen if you need anything, Philippe."

The other man appeared prepared to object.

But thankfully he thought better and moved out of Drew's way as he followed Josie to the kitchen. Drew didn't miss Philippe's lethal look though, that conveyed all that Philippe would have said and done if Josie hadn't appeared.

As he walked behind her, Drew couldn't keep from taking in the gentle, unconscious sway of Josie's hips and the sexy curve of her neck. But he had no place appreciating her pure grace when inside he felt so impure, as though a tar-like stain spread under his skin. A dread that all they'd begun to build between them was forever lost.

As much as he wished otherwise, Drew knew that this meeting in the kitchen wouldn't have anything to do with food and Josie being enjoyed on top of the island.

He expected her to turn toward him when they entered, but instead she busied herself making coffee.

"Talk," she said.

Josie's heart was beating so hard she thought for sure he could see it through her chest.

When Detective Chevalier had spilled what he knew, she hadn't wanted to believe he was telling her the truth. It didn't fit in with anything she knew about Drew or with what had happened between them.

But as the homicide detective had continued talking, verifying that the tip had been phoned into his office by an anonymous source who had nothing to gain, and that some checking had proven that Drew wasn't a car-parts salesman but rather an independent contractor who'd been dubbed "The Closer" by those he worked with, she'd had the sinking sensation that Chevalier was right.

Drew had always seemed a step above the

salesmen she usually crossed paths with. A little too well groomed. A little too edgy.

And now…

Well, the instant she'd glanced into his eyes, she'd known the information was right. And that he knew that she knew.

She quirked a brow at him over her shoulder only to find his gaze lingering on her backside.

Her blood heated, but not in anger. Instead, desire ignited in her stomach and rushed through her veins. A reaction she was sorely unprepared for.

How could she still crave him sexually when he'd hit her with such a crushing emotional blow?

"Josie, I…you have to believe me when I say that the last thing I want to do is hurt you."

He surely couldn't be saying what he was.

She turned fully and leaned against the counter while the coffee brewed. The only sounds were the spitting of the machine and the uneven cadence of her own heartbeat in her ears.

Her voice was quieter than she meant it to be. "Is this where you try to convince me that you only had my best interests in mind?" She swallowed past the emotion clogging her throat. "Drew, you…you wanted to take away the Josephine. My hotel."

Pain rippled across his handsome face. "I used the present tense, not the past."

She tried to follow him but her brain seemed oversaturated, incapable of making sense out of even the simplest of statements, and his had been anything but.

He looked suddenly agitated, as if understanding that he stood on a sinking boat that was taking on more water than he could bail out. And stunningly, she felt a need to make things easier for him.

How could that be? This man had come to her place under false pretenses, had lied to her from the word go. Had schemed to take away the thing that meant the most to her.

Hot tears flooded her eyes.

"I don't know what I'm doing here," she whispered, starting for the door so she could go up to her rooms and lock herself in where no one could bother her. No one could touch her. Lie to her.

She hadn't expected him to grasp her wrist as she passed. In a knee-jerk reaction, she slapped him soundly across the face with her free hand.

He blinked at her, and she got the impression that his wince was as much due to the physical blow as to the crack to his ego.

"I suppose I deserved that."

"You deserve much worse."

He averted his gaze. "You're right, I do."

Josie didn't know how she knew, but she sensed

that he meant what he was saying. And hope lit anew in her stomach.

A hope she didn't want. Not when what they'd shared had been temporary anyway. She'd always known it would end.

For some reason, she didn't want it to end badly.

He looked up into her eyes again, his gaze intense. "I know all this—what you've learned about me— is a shock. And that right now you're reacting on an emotional level…and that you're hurting." He lifted his hand to her face and stroked her cheek with his thumb. When she moved so he couldn't touch her, he dropped his hand back to his side, his eyes beseeching. "Think about it, Josie. Try to look beyond how you're feeling right now." She heard the click of his deep swallow. "Not once did I ever mention a word to you about selling the hotel. Not ever."

She couldn't fully absorb his words.

"What do you think that means, Josie? Here I am, a guy whose only intention, supposedly, is to get you to sell, yet I never mentioned the hotel and the many problems you're having. Not once."

From a place outside herself, she realized he was right. He'd never made the hotel or her ownership or possible sale of it the focus of any conversation they'd had.

Of course, most of their time together had been spent having sex.

Still…

She reached beyond the cloud of betrayal and hurt and tried to grasp something that was just outside her ability to get hold of just then.

"'The Closer,'" she whispered. "I get the impression you're very good at your job, Drew. At whatever you decide that job to be."

He shifted on his feet and she noticed the way he held his hands tightly still, as if barely able to contain his longing to touch her. And suddenly, irrationally, she wanted that touch more than her next breath, despite her knowledge that he could be working her still, even at this moment.

His voice lowered to a rasping murmur that made her shiver. "If you can't answer the question of why I never mentioned the hotel, Josie, then answer this one—what am I doing here? Why am I standing before you right now, out of my mind with the thought that I'll never again be able to touch you? Kiss you? Taste your sweetness on my tongue? Hold you in my arms?"

She searched his eyes, her brain stalling, her body longing to surge forward, longing for him. But she had more to say. "You could be here because you didn't finish what you came here to do."

She watched his eyes close briefly. Then he lifted his right hand, put it down again, then raised it again so that he could trail his fingertips over the inside of her arm at her elbow. Goose bumps ran over her skin at the subtle yet powerful touch. Over her wrist, her palm, then he was lacing his fingers with hers. He lifted her hand so that the back of it rested against his chest.

"You're right," he said. "I didn't finish what I started." His pupils dilated, taking over the blue of his eyes. "Only my objective did a complete one-eighty the instant I kissed you. The moment you invited me into your body...and into your heart."

The aforementioned organ had contracted to the point where it clutched painfully in her chest.

"And I am there, aren't I, Josie?" He moved their hands so that they rested between her breasts. "Just as you're in mine."

A part of her didn't want to hear what he was saying. Wanted words that would feed the ache in her stomach and help her shore up her crumbling defenses.

"Yes, I'm an independent contractor. Yes, I worked for a client that wants your hotel. Yes, I came here with the sole intention of getting it for him."

She narrowed her eyes. Where was he going

with this? Every word seemed to aim for and hit her where she was most vulnerable.

"But all that's changed, Josie. None of that makes sense to me anymore. My job seems so unimportant."

She licked her lips, unable to speak, unable to move, mesmerized by what he appeared to be saying.

"What is important is the fact that I'm falling in love with you."

An almost unbearable pain mixed with hope inside her.

"Correction—I'm not falling in love with you. I'm in love with you. And falling deeper every moment I gaze into your eyes and touch your soft skin."

His thumb was stroking her hand, sending sensations rushing up her arm and over her sleep-deprived body.

"I can't..." she began, towing her gaze from his face and searching for something, anything, with which to pull herself free from the overwhelming emotions enveloping her. "I can't deal with this right now, Drew." She found a piece of strength within to draw from. Strength that had been in the Villefranche family for longer, much longer, than she'd been a part of it. "Maybe what you're telling me is the truth. Maybe not. Maybe this is all just some sort of ruse to try to salvage a situation beyond repair."

On a level she was loath to recognize, she sensed that this wasn't the case, but her doubts needed to be addressed.

She smiled sadly, giving in to her own overpowering need to touch him and lifting her free hand to his face. She ran her fingertips over his strong cheekbone, over his jaw, the rasp of his stubble rough against her palm.

"Look," she whispered, focusing her attention on his mouth rather than his eyes. "We both knew that this, whatever it is that exists between us, was temporary. That it would end almost as quickly as it began." The prospect of not seeing him again hurt her more than what had transpired in the past few hours. What did that mean?

"Yes, but I'm not gone yet," he murmured.

Then he leaned in and did what she wanted most in the world in that one moment.

He kissed her.

16

DREW KNEW AN ALL-CONSUMING relief as he softly kissed Josie's sweet lips. She didn't resist. Moreover, she appeared to want the contact as much as he did.

Dear God, he didn't know what he'd done to deserve this chance, but he wasn't about to screw it up now.

He ran his thumb along her cheek then entwined his fingers in her dark, silky curls, pressing her nearer to him. She smelled like heaven and tasted even better.

Finally, she turned her head slightly, crushing her nose against the side of his neck, her breathing rapid and shallow.

"I need…time," she whispered.

Time was something neither one of them had, judging by everything he'd learned during his research.

But time was what he had to give her. He owed it to her. Even though he knew that with a few expert touches she'd writhe, needing and wanting, under his power.

"Okay."

He stepped away from her. Not far. A mere few inches. But she blinked at him as if he'd moved across the room.

"How long…"

She looked away, as if the beginning of the question she'd been about to ask wasn't one she wanted to hear the answer to.

"How much longer am I staying?"

She nodded, although she still avoided his gaze.

"I leave tomorrow."

Her eyes flooded with pain as she stared at him.

"Not for good. I have some things I have to see to. Some business matters."

She bit her bottom lip, her hand going to the side of her neck. "Related to the Josephine?"

"In a manner of speaking."

She didn't say anything for long moments.

"No more secrets, Drew. Please."

He groaned inwardly, wishing he could erase the hurt from her lovely face.

"Just one more."

Because in the past few minutes with her, witnessing her generous spirit and heart, realizing she was forgiving him even though she hadn't said the words, he decided not to tell her what he was doing. He didn't want her to refuse what she would certainly see as an act of charity. Instead, he felt that incredible desire to take care of her again. To move heaven and earth to get her what she wanted. And she wanted this hotel. No matter how battered. No matter the ghosts that walked the halls. No matter the darkness that lurked in the shadows.

He realized that he could just as easily have been describing Josie herself and his own need for her.

He took the card from the Marriott from his shirt pocket on which he'd scribbled his cell phone number. "My flight leaves in the morning." He took her hand, turned it palm up, then placed the card there before putting his fingers over them both.

He didn't say anything more. Didn't have to. They both knew that the act of his giving her the card meant it was up to her if she wanted to see him. All she had to do was call.

Drew leaned forward and pressed his lips to her temple, breathing in the fresh, sexy scent of her. Then he turned and walked away, even though it killed him to think that it might be for the last time.

JOSIE STAYED IN THE KITCHEN by herself for a long time after Drew had left her. She'd drifted to a stool at the island where their love affair had begun a few short days before. She wanted to believe what Drew had told her. Wanted it with every cell in her body, every breath she took in.

She was so preoccupied with her thoughts, trying to work everything out, she didn't hear someone come in.

"Uh-huh. You got it bad, girl."

Josie blinked Anne-Marie into focus, an exasperated Philippe standing next to her.

"What…"

She was going to ask what Anne-Marie was doing there, but didn't get the words out before deciding Philippe had probably contacted her.

Josie got up from the stool and continued making coffee for herself, including cups for her two friends. By the time she was done, they were both sitting at the cutting board.

"Is it true?" Anne-Marie asked. "Was Morrison here to get you to sell the Josephine?"

Josie nodded as she took a deep sip from her coffee.

"I knew it. I knew there was something about him. Something that kept coming up in the cards. Mystery. Deception."

"So what did he say?" Philippe asked. "Did he come here to finish the job?"

She remembered what Drew had said about his intentions having changed and smiled softly. "No."

"But he tried."

"Yes. But not in the way you think." She put her cup down. "It had nothing to do with the hotel."

"Maybe it should have." Anne-Marie drank from her own cup, causing her bracelets to clank.

"How so?"

Her friend shook her dark head, which was covered with the usual African head wrap. "Josie, I hate to be the one to tell you this, but this place, the Josephine, is packed full of bad karma." She looked around as if half-afraid an entity might materialize from out of thin air and go for her throat. "It's all I can do to sit here with you."

Josie absorbed her words. "Are you telling me I should sell?"

Anne-Marie's eyes were sober. "I'm saying that maybe you should consider it."

Josie felt as if the ceiling had just fallen in on her.

The one person she'd expected to try to talk her into giving up the Josephine—Drew—hadn't, while her best friend, a woman she'd known for countless years, who knew how much the hotel was a part of her, was.

The day was beginning to emerge as one of the most unpredictable of her life.

She looked at Philippe, who was considering his coffee.

"Maybe she's right, Jos."

She couldn't believe she was hearing this. She moved to get up from the table.

Anne-Marie placed a stilling hand on her arm. "We're just concerned about you, girl. We see how much you have on your shoulders. You've been carrying quite a burden since your *granme* passed to the other side and it's only gotten heavier since the murders." She shook her head. "I say maybe you should take what they're offering and run. Start up a new life someplace else. Somewhere that isn't as haunted by the past as this place is."

A part of her recognized that what they were saying was right. Another felt betrayed for the second time that day.

She met Anne-Marie's pitying gaze. "I want you to help me rid the hotel of that bad karma," she said point-blank.

Her comment appeared to be the last thing either of them had expected her to say.

She'd surprised even herself.

"If it's true that this place is cursed, then you're just the person to help me, right?"

Anne-Marie didn't appear to know what to say. "I thought you didn't buy into any of that."

"At this point, I'm just about willing to try anything."

Philippe made a tsk-tsking sound and got up to refresh his coffee, topping off Josie's cup as well, while Anne-Marie appeared to ponder what Josie was asking.

"You can't just try, chérie. You must believe."

"Believe in the ritual?"

"Believe that good can conquer evil. That love triumphs over all."

Love…

Anne-Marie's gaze narrowed on her. Then she appeared to come to some sort of understanding, while Josie felt like the other woman had just gazed straight down into the very chamber of her heart.

Anne-Marie nodded. "Yes, yes. This just might work."

DREW PACED THE LENGTH of his room then back again. His suitcase was packed, as was his laptop.

He looked at his watch. Three hours had passed since he'd left Josie standing alone in the kitchen. Walking away from her had been, beyond a shadow of a doubt, the hardest thing he'd ever done. Harder than facing a battalion of heavily armed Iraqi soldiers on the border of Kuwait.

More difficult than his divorce. Tougher than his demotion when his divorce had delivered a blow he hadn't expected.

She wasn't going to call.

Shit.

But he hadn't been called "The Closer" for nothing. He'd be damned if he'd give in that easily.

Leaving his suitcase and briefcase sitting near the door, he went out into the hall, his intention to head over to the Josephine and do what he probably should have earlier. Kiss Josie until she remembered none of the bad and wanted nothing more than to enjoy more of the good.

His cell phone vibrated in his pocket. He slowed his purposeful stride down the hall and fished it out of his pants.

"Hello?"

"Drew?"

Josie.

He stopped and closed his eyes.

"If you're free, I'd like you to come over tonight. Say around ten?"

Ten. A good four hours away. He didn't think he could survive it.

But he would have to.

"I'll be there."

17

FOLLOWING THEIR CONVERSATION in the kitchen, Anne-Marie insisted that the first order of business was to scour room 2B. No cleansing ritual could be expected to work while the blood of a dead woman still marred the place, she'd said.

So she and Josie cleaned it. Top to bottom. Placing the stained mattress in the back alley, despite Detective Chevalier's instructions that neither guest room was to be touched since they'd been deemed crime scenes.

After they'd completed that somber task, Anne-Marie had gone back to her shop, promising to return shortly, while Philippe stayed in the kitchen to make dinner.

Josie, on the other hand, was in her rooms, once her grandmother's rooms, on the fourth floor.

She stood in the middle of her bedroom, looking around with eyes other than her own. While the additional rooms had always belonged to her grandmother, this one had been hers. It had changed over the years. From a twin canopy bed with pink accents, to a queen-size wrought-iron bed not unlike those in the guest rooms. Except it had a canopy with white sheers draped around the top posts, lending it what was supposed to be a romantic effect, but now only looked ghostly. Especially with the breeze blowing in from the open French doors, disturbing the gauzy fabric so that it billowed out, resembling a phantom.

She'd never had a man up here before. Had never had cause to because all her liaisons had been fleeting, carried out in the guest rooms where her lovers had stayed.

She reminded herself that Drew fell solidly into the same category, even if he was no longer staying at the hotel. Only she knew that the connection to him that dwelled within her, that grew every time he touched her, would be with her till the grave.

Gathering fresh linens from a nearby closet, she stripped the bed and remade it, fluffing the pillows on top. Then she took the white candles on black wrought-iron stands that were placed throughout the room and repositioned them on the nightstands on either side of the bed, careful to tuck the canopy sheers on the back board so they wouldn't accidentally catch fire.

Narcissus.

She thought she smelled the unique, indigenous fragrance on the night air. The unmistakable scent her grandmother always wore. She turned her head, trying to identify the source of the smell.

Then she did what she'd only done once, very briefly, in twelve months. She stepped out into the main drawing room and stood outside her grandmother's private rooms.

She'd breached Josephine Villefranche's sanctuary one other time since saying her final goodbyes a year ago. But she hadn't stayed long. Hadn't been able to. She'd only picked up the fan she used at the front desk that had been lying on her grandmother's rocking chair and then had quickly left.

She sniffed. The scent was stronger here.

Odd that she shouldn't have sensed it until now.

She gripped the doorknobs of the ornately carved double doors and slowly pushed them inward.

As impossible as it seemed, a gust of fresh air hit her head-on, blowing her black curls from around her face and infusing her with the smell of narcissus, as though an entity not of this world had just traveled through her. She stared unblinkingly at the familiar room, half expecting her grandmother to materialize in front of her, looking for her usual kiss on the cheek.

Of course, she didn't appear. But Josie felt her presence everywhere. Smelled it. Sensed it.

She slowly stepped from one familiar object to another. From an old oval picture frame that held a shot of *Granme* with her two young daughters, the girls looking as different from each other as night and day. To the wooden rocking chair that still held Josephine's favorite shawl. To the bed that Josie had left made as if her grandmother might want to use it some night.

The source of the narcissus came from the wrought-iron dressing table. She stepped to it, picked up a crystal spray bottle and squeezed the decanter so that a fine mist filled the air. Immediately she was enveloped in everything that was her grandmother.

"Remember, always, that you are only as beautiful as you feel," she'd said to her while Josie had sat in the rocker watching her grandmother get ready for church one Sunday morning. "And smell."

She sat down on the bed, the same bed that when she'd first arrived at the hotel, she'd spent sleeping in with her grandmother to help chase away the nightmares that abandonment had caused. She ran her hand over the meticulously tatted lace.

It seemed like a long time later when she finally got up and left the room, closing the doors after herself.

And it was only then that she realized she still held the bottle of perfume.

THREE HOURS LATER, Josie again stood alone in her room. Night had long since fallen. Anne-Marie was long gone. But the rituals Josie had helped her perform remained in her mind and likely always would.

She remembered a time long ago when her mother had dabbled in white magic, the voodoo. Lighting candles and sitting for long hours watching the flame grow lower. But while it was rumored her great grandmother had been a witch of sorts, her grandmother had never bought into it and had refused to allow Josie to be tempted down that route. She'd infused the Church in her instead, making sure she went to services every Sunday and that she prayed before going to bed every night when she was younger.

Of course, Josie had been surrounded by voodoo her entire life. Her best friend owned one shop out of the dozens that catered to interest in the occult. And Josie had been in that shop count-less times. But she'd always looked upon it as something to make her smile. She'd never taken it seriously, dismissing the rituals as strange, the beliefs as unworthy.

But as she'd watched Anne-Marie bring herself to a oneness with the four elements and, using natural herbs and oils, cleanse the hotel, she saw there was nothing hokey or damaging about the ritual. In fact, the mere act of participating had brought her a sense of peace and awareness of her surroundings that she hadn't felt in a long, long time.

When Anne-Marie had finished with the hotel, she'd commanded Josie to kneel over the bathtub in her private bathroom and went about pouring an aromatic wash over her hair and head several times before filling the tub and asking her to soak in it.

The final ritual, Anne-Marie had said, was one only Josie herself could perform. Setting up a table in the middle of the private sitting room, Anne-Marie had draped a white cloth over it then placed a single white candle in the middle.

Even now, wearing a loose-fitting, white gauzy dressing gown her friend had given her, Josie sat in front of the table, concentrating on the flame, the scent of sage and various oils teasing her senses, the sweetness of narcissus just beyond.

"Clear your mind of everything," Anne-Marie had told her. "Focus only on the color white. And imagine yourself pushing that whiteness on everything around you, from the inside out, up to and including the hotel, until you reach the front curb."

Her friend had smiled at her softly then, a serenity on her face that Josie couldn't help absorbing. She didn't have to say aloud that she had gotten it. She suspected that was as obvious on her face as it had been on her friend's.

She didn't hope that the rituals would work. She *knew* they would…

THE HOTEL WAS NOTABLY QUIET given the sound of the raucous jazz streaming from the bar across the street. Drew hesitated in front of the open door, looking up the lit street. The blind horn player had taken up his spot on the corner again, blowing a tune that made its way under Drew's skin so that the trumpet was the only thing he heard outside his own heartbeat.

He didn't know how this was going to turn out. Josie had been matter-of-fact on the phone earlier when she'd asked him to come tonight. He stepped inside the lobby, the scent of sage unusually strong. He looked around, finding different-sized white candles burning in every corner and forming a line that went even into the courtyard and the kitchen beyond.

He felt another well of fear that this meeting would be a quiet send-off, a "nice to meet you, too bad you turned out to be a louse" chat that would leave him standing on the street alone wondering what had happened. It didn't help that even he believed it was no less than he deserved.

But, somehow, the atmosphere inside the hotel also infused him with something else. Hope, perhaps, that he might have a chance to prove that his feelings for Josie went deeper than his deception.

"Josie?" he quietly called.

There was no answer. Not from Josie or Philippe, whom, he assumed, she'd let go for the night.

Drew glanced at the door behind himself, wondering if he should close it. But there was something that urged him to leave it open, a cross breeze he hadn't noticed before that seemed to flow from the top of the building to the bottom, enveloping him where he stood. The scent of something exotically floral teased his nose, seeming to draw his attention to the stairs.

He squinted at the candles placed on each of the steps, then started to climb, first to the second floor, then following the flickering wicks up to the third, then the fourth, a place he'd never visited before.

All the doors stood open. He wasn't sure how he knew to walk straight ahead rather than go into either of the open doorways to his right and left, but he halted just outside the third one. He blinked, sure he was seeing things. Seated in front of a table was Josie, her golden skin shiny and beautiful, contrasting against the sheer white dress she wore. She appeared to be in some sort of trance, the planes of her face relaxed and peaceful. She looked exactly like the enchantress he'd once thought her.

Drew stood mesmerized as the flame of the candle on the table in front of her flickered, playing hide-and-seek with the shadows. She blinked, as if having been alerted to his presence, then looked up into his face and smiled.

Drew felt like she'd touched him although she sat a good twenty feet away.

She slowly rose to her feet and rounded the table, seeming to float more than walk. When she stepped in front of the candle, he saw how very sheer the dress she wore was. Her luscious body was clearly outlined and he could make out the dusty rounds of her areolae and the deep V of curls between her thighs.

He swallowed hard as she came to stop in front of him.

"I'm glad you came," she said quietly.

Glad didn't begin to cover how he felt about being

there, present in her private rooms, gaining a glimpse into a woman who'd fascinated him since the beginning. He felt honored, undeserving and awed.

He thought of all the things that he wanted to say. That he'd put together in his mind over the past four hours since her phone call. There was a proposition that he wanted to make, that covered both personal and business matters. And he'd composed an expanded explanation for his deceptive actions.

He remembered the call he'd made to his client. His final call, because he'd used the opportunity to quit. Something that hadn't gone over very well and had resulted in a lot of threats that involved him never working in this business again.

He'd expected the reaction, but had never anticipated the venom that had gone along with it. After all, he was dropping a client, not taking one of Rove's children hostage.

Drew hadn't realized how very off balance his life had been until that one moment. How much importance he and those he worked for placed on their business pursuits to the exclusion of all else.

A game. That's what it all was. Some sort of pointless, intense match of wills that required your complete attention. Forget family or home or personal enjoyment or conscience. It was all about the next deal, the next kill, the money involved.

Never mind what you did with the money. Whether you enjoyed the results of your labor. That didn't matter. What did was getting it. Period.

And Josie, with her soft smile, had made him realize that that was no longer enough.

She held out her hand and he took it, marveling at the smoothness of her skin. No matter how much he wanted to haul her into his arms and kiss the life out her, he found he could do little more than follow her lead, allow her to call the shots.

And he had little doubt that whatever happened tonight would be something he would never forget.

_18_

"ALLOW YOURSELF TO FEEL the love, Josie. Love is the true genesis of all things good. No bad can hide from love."

Anne-Marie's parting words echoed in Josie's mind as she reached out, filling her, lifting her, making her feel outside herself. Her heart floated in her chest, her stomach felt fathomless, and every cell, every throb of her pulse, was aware of the man standing opposite her.

Gone from her mind was his deception. Banished was any thought of this night being their last time together. Nowhere in sight were the problems she was having. All that existed in that one moment in time was love. Her love for Drew. And, yes, she realized, his love for her as well.

Rather than turning away from the raw emotion so clearly etched on his handsome face, she reveled in it. He loved her. It was there in the dark blue depth of his eyes. If she placed a hand on his chest, she felt sure she'd feel it in the heat of his heart. A heart he'd opened to her as surely as she'd opened hers to him. While she hadn't been aware of what was happening at the time, now that she did know, rather than closing the door, she opened it, drawing from the extraordinary emotion, allowing it to dictate her thoughts, her actions.

"Come," she said softly, leading him to the open door of her bedroom.

The candles burned on the nightstands, giving an otherworldly feel to the room. The air coming in through the open French doors flickered the flames and stirred the sheers on the canopy.

Josie stopped at the foot of the bed then turned to face Drew again. He had yet to say anything, and she didn't need him to. Everything that needed to be expressed would come through action rather than words.

She released his hands then crossed her arms in front of her breasts as she reached up to her shoulders. She brushed the light material down over her shoulders, baring one at a time. Drew watched her movement as she caught the fabric between her breasts. But she didn't use it to cover herself. Rather her nipples stood out, prominent and proud, and then she allowed the sheath to pool around her feet on the floor.

She watched Drew swallow and she read what he couldn't say. He found her beautiful. And she felt beautiful. Wanted. Wanton.

He moved, unbuttoning his shirt as if on automatic pilot, his gaze never leaving hers as the soft cotton rasped from his skin to join her sheath on the floor. The whisper of a zipper later, his slacks and boxers followed suit, his need for her evident in the erection that seemed to reach out for her.

Josie slowly curved her fingers around his turgid flesh, watching as his pupils dilated and his breath came out in a rush. So thick. So hard. So hot. She explored the silken shaft with her fingertips, finding a bead of moisture on the engorged knob. Her mouth watered with the desire to taste him, to feel him against her tongue. She slid down to one knee, then the other, until her mouth was mere millimeters in front of his arousal.

Drew still hadn't moved. He stood stock-still, watching her as she cupped his sac, reveling in the feel of his coarse pubic hair against her palm. She kissed his erection, then swirled her tongue over the tip, lapping up the moisture there even as she added a different type of moisture with her mouth. Then she fitted her lips around the end, creating a wet channel with her tongue, and took in as much of his considerable length as she could, withdrawing when she reached that point, then starting over again.

She felt his flesh pulsate and grow thicker. Sensed his growing urgency from the stiffness of his body and the rapidness of his breathing. She gently squeezed his sac, then moved her fingertips to just beyond, to the nerve system there, and pressed the knotted flesh, holding off his crisis even as she slid her mouth to cover him again.

He tasted sweet and sour, hot and hard. And she couldn't seem to get enough of him as she licked and suckled and squeezed.

Finally, he moved.

She felt his hands on her bare shoulders and understood he was urging her to stand up before him. His face was savage with need. His fingers indented the flesh of her hips as he curved them around to her backside, cupping her bottom. Then he lifted her so that her legs went around his hips and she felt his hardness pressing against her slick softness.

Josie's heart seemed to stop and expand and beat harder all at once. She balanced herself with her hands on his shoulders, her gaze locked with his. Then he slid his hands down further from behind, his fingers finding the tight bud nestled in her curls. She lost her breath as he pressed it. Then he parted her swollen labia, testing her readiness, the proof of her arousal covering his fingers, lubricating them so that they easily slid inside her tight canal.

Josie's eyelids drifted closed as she rode the swell of white-hot sensation.

Then he replaced his fingers with the head of his shaft. Slowly, torturously, he moved her down until she covered him fully, her pubis resting against his, her curls entangled with his. Bare flesh meeting bare flesh.

Josie pulled air deep into her lungs, her tingling breasts lifting until they brushed the fine hair sprinkling his chest. She grasped on a deeper level the significance of their joining without protection. The trust inherent in such a move touched her beyond words, beyond understanding. Everything that was her seemed to fuse with him, throbbing, expanding and contracting, their heartbeats one as she crossed her ankles behind his back and lifted herself up from his shaft, then slowly slid back down.

He was kissing her. Gently at first, one hand supporting her bottom, the other curving around to the back of her head, holding her still as he launched a sensuous assault. His tongue flicked over her bottom lip then dipped inside her mouth. Her hunger growing, she wrapped her arms around his neck, entangling her fingers in his hair, pressing her breasts fully against his chest, her nipples hypersensitive.

He slid his hands to her waist, taking his time. Gripping her hips, he lifted her up, then back down, establishing an easy, deep rhythm that made her quake from the inside out as she squeezed and released the tension of her legs to accommodate the move. She leaned back so that only her fingers were laced behind his neck, encouraging an even deeper meeting. Then she swiveled her hips, rubbing provocatively against him.

He groaned, his erection twitching inside her when she did it again. Then again, her own crisis growing nearer as she watched the effect she was having on him. Moisture dotted his forehead, dampening the hair that had fallen over his brow, drawing attention to the desire darkening his eyes. Then she released her grip on his neck…

Drew knew a moment of fear when Josie let go of him, knowing that she wouldn't be able to support herself. He shifted his balance to protect her…only it appeared she knew exactly what she was doing. Clasping her hands tightly over his at her hips, she leaned back, farther and farther, until she could touch the floor. The view the move provided sent his blood pressure soaring: his member buried deep inside her, her pink flesh engorged and glistening in the candlelight.

She released his hands then stretched her arms over her head, bracing herself against the floor and tightening her legs behind him. Then she moved.

Drew's heart beat thickly as his hips bucked, once, twice, then he was releasing his seed in her slick, tight opening at the same time her own passion-filled moan filled his ears.

For long moments, he was incapable of movement, his knees threatening to give way under the sudden weakness. He felt Josie's hands on his again, and he grasped them, lifting her until he held her tight against his chest. She released her legs and slid down the length of him, the mere feel of skin against skin enough to make his erection twitch back to life.

Then she kissed him.

Dear Lord but this woman was going to be the end of him. She tasted of sweetness, and heat and desire, her lips claiming his in gentle persuasion. But what she was trying to persuade him of, he didn't know. Surely she knew that he loved her? Was she perhaps attempting to get him to say it? He gazed deep into her eyes and knew that she wasn't. Instead, she seemed to be saying the words herself.

The realization nearly knocked him over with the power of it. Deepening the kiss, he swept her up into his arms and carried her to the canopy bed, laying her gently across the length of it. Then he followed, covering her body with his, doing nothing more than kissing her and somehow feeling that if he could do that for the rest of his life, he'd never want for anything more.

The sound of the trumpet grew almost mournful as it drifted through the open doors. The candlelight flickered over her, her exotic beauty dark against the white linens and pillows. After long minutes, he trailed his fingers down over her defined collarbone, over the damp skin between her breasts, over her toned stomach. Reaching her moist curls, he nudged her open with his index finger and thumb. He dipped into her slick channel, then used the proof of their desire to swirl his fingertip around her tight nub. Her back arched against the mattress, thrusting her breasts into the air. He hungrily claimed them, taking each into his mouth as he caressed her below, licking and drawing them deep until they were shiny from his attention. Then he thrust two fingers deep inside her waiting flesh, drawing her muscles tight.

After riding the wave of sensation caused by his move, she looked at him with her whiskey-brown eyes. The raw emotion there stopped him in his tracks. And touched him more profoundly than any physical act. The honesty…the naked-ness…the power was almost too much for him to view head-on.

So he didn't.

Instead, he smoothed his hands over her lithe body, then coaxed her to roll over onto her stomach. She rose up onto her knees until her sex was in contact with his sex again. She stretched her hands straight out in front of herself, elongating her back as she strained back against him. He ran his thumbs the length of her spine and gasped when he felt one of her hands grasp his erection between her legs and place his knob against her. Then she slid back, taking him in.

Drew instinctually bucked in response, thrust-ing himself even deeper. And as he moved in and out, watching her juices flood over his turgid flesh, he realized that he hadn't used protection.

The thought caused him a moment of pause. He'd never gone without protection. Not even while married because Carol hadn't wanted to go on the pill. Something about weight gain and risks that he didn't understand. And since he'd never even come close to having the children conversa-tion with her, he'd always worn condoms.

But now…

Josie drew away then rolled over onto her back, placing her legs on either side of his as she gazed up at him.

And in that one moment, Drew knew that he'd be the luckiest man in the world if the woman, this woman, who had rocked his life to the core, would be the mother of his child.

When he reentered, he didn't turn away, didn't mask his emotions, and he met hers head-on.

A FEW HOURS LATER, Josie roused from a light sleep, her bottom snuggled against Drew's hip where he lay on his back next to her. A few of the candles had burned themselves out, leaving the room dimmer than it had been earlier. But the light that filled her was more than enough compensation.

She'd never experienced before what they'd shared tonight. Now she understood what it meant to truly make love. And she wondered how anyone could ever compare cold, emotionless sex with what she and Drew had just shared.

The scent of their mixed passion filled her senses and her chest felt as if it were packed with cotton batting, as weightless as a cloud. Longing and need filled her on an emotional level as powerfully as physical desire, and she was loath to examine it too closely for fear that it might vanish.

She heard Drew's even breathing catch, then he rolled over, placing his front against her back. Her womanhood was swollen to almost the point of pain from his passionate attentions, but that didn't stop her from wanting him all over again.

She turned and slid her right leg over his, rubbing herself wantonly against his growing arousal. His hand moved over her stomach, causing her to catch her breath as his fingers burrowed into her curls and fondled her at the same time as he entered her again.

Heat spread through her limbs, and she tilted her hips back and forth in time with his leisurely strokes, his fingers keeping pace against her. She reached down between them and caressed his balls, pressing them against her clit then encircling the base of his penis as he entered her then exited.

She loved every moment of their joining. It fascinated her. He fascinated her. She didn't think she would ever tire of discovering the things that mildly stimulated him and the ones that shoved him right over the edge. While she enjoyed touching their joined parts, following the movements, he liked to watch. She thought of climbing back on top of him so he could do just that when a sudden climax caught her off guard. He came at the same time she did.

He slowly stroked her until her spasms subsided, drawing her closer against him, despite the heat.

"Water," he whispered against her ear. "I need water."

She moved to get up.

"No. You stay here. I'll go get it."

She lay back, lazily watching as he got up and his tight butt disappeared into the connecting bath. A moment later he came back out with a towel secured around his hips, grinning her way, then going out into the hall through the drawing room. Soon thereafter, she heard his footfalls on the steps.

Josie closed her eyes and realized she was smiling. She idly drew her fingertips along the length of her stomach, then back again, then trailed a path to her own womanhood. She wanted to cup herself, as if the action could somehow trap Drew's sperm inside her.

She stretched her neck. Is this what her grandmother and mother had done with their lovers when they'd conceived? Had they been with men they loved, but knew they couldn't have except in one important way? Had they thrown caution to the wind, praying for a child out of the most moving experience of their lives?

The thought that Drew's sperm was even now making its way toward one of her eggs made her chest feel lighter still.

A sound made her open her eyes.

Only it wasn't Drew standing gazing at her from the open doorway.

It was Philippe.

19

DREW WASN'T SURE what had hit him. All he knew was that when he opened a bleary eye, he was lying facedown first on the kitchen floor, the tile cool against his cheek.

He felt the back of his head, his fingers coming away with dark liquid. Damn, but that hurt.

He attempted to get up, only to feel the floor shift under him again and force him back down. Oh, boy. This wasn't good. He remembered the open front door.

Josie…

JOSIE WAS INSTANTLY AWARE of how open she was to the man looking at her as if he had a right to. Her legs were spread, her breasts bare.

She quickly lifted to a sitting position and pulled the top sheet to cover herself.

"Philippe! What are you doing here?"

She smoothed her hand over her hair, looking around.

"Has something happened? Is something wrong?"

He hadn't answered her and his silence made her heartbeat kick up a notch.

She started to get up from the bed, suddenly not comfortable in the prone position while he continued to look at her. "Jesus, Philippe, what's going on?"

Before she could stand, he was knocking her back down on the bed.

Josie gasped, struggling to turn to face him, but he seemed just as determined to keep her face-down, his weight threatening against her.

"You just wouldn't do what I wanted you to do, would you, Josie?" he asked, his voice low and menacing.

Fear quick and sure spread through her with alarming rapidity.

"What are you talking about?" She fought to keep the panic out of her voice. "Philippe, let me go, for God's sake."

He chuckled into her ear but there was no humor in the sound. "Oh, no, Josie. You don't get to tell me what to do anymore."

She felt the evidence of his arousal against her bottom. Bile rose up in her throat.

"I...I don't understand," she said. "What have you asked me to do that I didn't do?" She knew she was grasping at straws, but she needed to understand why someone she had thought her friend was attacking her in her own bed.

She thought of Drew down in the kitchen. Surely, he should have returned by now. Had Philippe done something—

"You wouldn't sell the Josephine."

The warmth disappeared from Josie's blood.

"That's right. That's the whole reason I was here. Why I ever took a job in this godforsaken place. I was hired to convince you to sell to Dick Rove."

The name on the envelopes that arrived every week like clockwork.

"But no, you wouldn't listen to reason. Even as you sank deeper into debt, you held on to this hole-in-the-wall dump."

He moved to strip the sheet from her body while still holding her down.

"God damn it, Philippe, what are you doing?" She thrashed against him, alarm growing. "You're gay."

Again the laugh.

"Rape is about power, Josie. Not sex." She fought to hold on to the sheet as he struggled to take it from her. "Not that I am gay, mind you. I just knew that when Samuel died, you would be leery of strangers. An easygoing gay guy who still lived with his mother seemed to be just what you were in the market for." His words sounded closer to her ear. "Well, I don't live with my mother. And, as you're about to find out, I'm not gay."

Josie wasn't capable of hearing his words. She was all too aware that she was losing the battle with the sheet and that given his larger size and greater strength, she would be no match against him.

He shoved her face into the linens and she squeezed her eyes shut, trying not to think about how he was about to sully the beauty of what she and Drew had spent the night doing.

Blindly, she reached a hand out in front of herself. Her heart filled with hope when she felt the edge of the end table, then the base of a candleholder. Grasping it, and praying that the wick was still burning, she swung it in his direction.

He made a shrill sound and then his hands were no longer on her.

Josie struggled immediately to the other side of the bed and off, glancing over to see melted wax from the candle cooling on his face. He swiped at it, his eyes closed.

The sheet was twisted under his knees so she left it, snatching the sheath she'd been wearing earlier from the floor as she bolted for the door and out into the drawing room beyond. She heard an inhuman roar, then Philippe was crashing against her, toppling her to the floor and taking the table holding the single white candle with them.

"You just don't know when to give up, do you?" he growled.

He roughly turned her over and tried to force her legs open with his knee.

"This place is falling down around your ears, not even prostitutes want to stay here, except that dead bitch Frederique, and yet there you are, still determined to make it."

He thrust his hand against her throat, choking off air and causing her to cough. But his mention of Frederique sparked a memory. He'd opted out of cleaning room 2B earlier, claiming that someone needed to man the front desk.

Could he have killed Frederique? Unlike the general public, he had full knowledge of how the first victim, Claire Laraway had been murdered, right down to how she'd been positioned on the bed. Had he orchestrated a copycat killing, taking care of two birds with one stone by doing away with someone helping Josie and guaranteeing the scandal would chase away any others thinking about staying there?

It seemed so far-fetched.

Then again, what he was doing right now would have seemed the same ten minutes ago.

Her throat burned from the pressure he applied. She started coughing hard, tears coming to her eyes.

Strangely, he loosened his grip slightly. Josie dragged in deep breaths of air.

"Frederique," she croaked. "What did you do to her?"

The candle on the table they'd overturned during their fall ignited the white tablecloth. The flash of yellow light threw his features into relief as he grinned at her malevolently. "The same that I'm about to do to you."

The Quarter Killer.

Was it possible that Philippe had committed both the murders of Claire Laraway and Frederique? But Claude had indicated that even though the murders had the same MO on the surface, there were many differences. The first being the rape. The second, the choice of weapon. Claire's throat had been cut with a clean-edged knife, while Frederique's flesh had been roughly slit with a duller blade.

Philippe was again trying to pry Josie's legs apart despite the growing yellow ball of flame to her right. The burning tablecloth had acted like a wick, leading the fire to the curtains. Peripherally, she saw one of the curtains burn from the support poll and land on the settee, where it would most likely set that afire as well.

The Josephine.

She fought against her captor doubly hard.

"Damn you, Philippe! Damn you. May you rot in hell for what you've done."

"What I've done is nothing compared to what I'm going to do."

She thrashed her legs, sending him off balance. "Your boss won't like it if you burn the place down."

"My boss will probably give me a bonus."

Josie's throat was raw with pain where he continued to grip her. "How much is he paying you? I'll double the amount."

His full-bodied laugh made her shudder. "With what, Josie? Your good looks?" His gaze scanned her naked frame. "It might have been tempting, once. But since I'm already going to take what you would have given me—"

"Money! I have money," she cried. "Lots of it."

His eyes narrowed. "Who's trying to con who now?"

"I'm telling the truth. I went to the bank today and took out a mortgage. The hotel was paid for, free and clear, and I took out a loan to help me get her back up and running again. To bridge the time between now and when business returns."

She'd also done a lot more to guarantee the Josephine's survival, but all he needed to know was that she had cash on hand. Lots of it.

"You're lying."

"On my grandmother's grave, I have it."

He released her neck. She tried to struggle up to a less vulnerable position.

"Where is it?"

"Downstairs. At the front desk."

He stared at her, apparently unaware of the fire that was growling next to them. "Liar. You wouldn't keep that kind of money downstairs with the doors open."

"Think about it. That's exactly where I would keep the money. Like you, that's the last place anyone would look for it."

He removed his weight and lifted her with a hand at the back of her neck. Josie gasped as he shoved her toward the door. She just managed to grab her white sheath before she was stumbling down the stairs. An ominous whoosh sounded behind her as the fire greedily ate everything in its path in her private rooms, fed by the air circulating through the hotel. Air that had been meant to cleanse the structure of any bad karma.

Air that was now helping in the destruction of the Josephine.

She'd managed to get the sheath over herself just as Philippe shoved her down the last remaining stairs into the lobby. She fought to keep her footing and ran for the desk and the shotgun that was behind it.

He caught the back of her hair, pulling hard. Hot tears flooded her eyes and shards of pain shot up her scalp. "Oh, no, you don't."

He shoved her to the side, keeping a hand on her as he procured the cash lockbox and the key for it that she kept in a drawer.

Josie used his distraction to edge a little closer to the desk, to the gun. As he awkwardly attempted to open the box with one hand, he released his grip on her slightly.

She took full advantage of the opportunity and shoved him to the side, grabbing for the gun she'd left unlocked.

It wasn't there…

A loud click sounded.

"Looking for this?" Drew said, the muzzle of the weapon pressed against Philippe's temple.

20

DREW'S HEAD HURT LIKE HELL and he didn't feel exactly threatening in the towel around his hips, but all that melted into the background in light of the scene before him. Philippe holding Josie by her soft curls, the white sheath she'd worn earlier hanging low to reveal her precious nakedness to the world.

"Release her. Now." He shoved the gun harder against the assistant manager's head.

Philippe let her go.

Drew knew a moment of relief so powerful he let his guard down.

Philippe went sailing over the desk, the lockbox in hand as he scrambled for the open door.

"Shoot him!" Josie shouted.

Drew stared at her. He remembered Dick Rove accusing him of being capable of murder. While his stint in the military had resulted in his share of gunfire, he knew the severity of the consequences.

Sirens sounded from somewhere in the distance.

"We know who he is now, Josie," he said quietly, putting the gun down as Philippe gained his footing. "The police will find him."

"The hell they will," she said, yanking the gun from his hands and taking aim.

Philippe turned at the door as if to give a triumphant grin before he disappeared into the crowded street beyond. And Josie squeezed the trigger, at the last second adjusting her aim so that she didn't hit him in the head and chest, but rather the groin.

It was enough to take the man down, screaming.

Josie dropped the gun to her side. "That's what you call Creole justice."

IT WAS SAID THAT PROBLEMS somehow looked better in the light of day. "Sleep on it, everything will look better in the morning," people said.

But this morning, everything looked worse.

Drew stood on the street a couple of buildings up from Hotel Josephine, an officer having given him a pair of uniform slacks and a T-shirt, though his feet were still bare. Josie was next to him in her sheath and a police blanket. The N.O. Fire Department was putting out the last of the flames

Drew hadn't even known had been raging on the fourth floor. Sooty water trickled through the lobby door and over the curb, making its way toward the sewer drain a ways down. What hadn't been burned had suffered major smoke and water damage.

A black cat rushed up from behind one of the two fire engines positioned in front of the hotel and wound around Josie's ankles, her legs bare but for the string of shells she always wore. She smiled at the cat then swept it up into her arms, rubbing its face against her cheek.

"Jez."

Drew was amazed at how much like a Caribbean priestess she looked in that one moment.

"Miss, do you have the address of the place you'll be staying?" a fire captain asked, taking off his hat and dragging the back of his hand across his brow.

"I'll be staying here," Josie said simply.

He shook his head. "This structure is uninhabitable. While you were lucky that only the fourth floor has burn damage, the place is a security risk until you can get someone in here for repairs."

"She'll be staying with me at the Marriott," Drew said.

The fireman nodded.

"No," Josie said, looking up the street at where her friend Anne-Marie was hurrying toward them. She immediately enveloped Josie in a hug, then got the abbreviated version of what had happened.

Philippe Murrell had been taken away in an ambulance, handcuffed to his gurney, an armed police officer along for the ride to the hospital and to the county jail after that. Not only had he been responsible for many of the problems Josie had encountered lately, including the voodoo rituals designed to scare her off, but it appeared he was to blame for the prostitute's murder, if not the killing of the first girl.

"I'll be staying with my friend," Josie said quietly when the fire captain cleared his throat.

Anne-Marie blinked, looked at Drew, then agreed. "Yes. Here's my contact info…"

Drew didn't hear the rest of what she said, namely because he was trying to work out why Josie had refused to stay with him.

His gaze met and locked with Josie's as she put the cat down.

He didn't understand. Had he done something wrong? The intimacy they'd shared, the connection they'd made…he couldn't have imagined it.

As he looked into Josie's liquid brown eyes, he

knew that he hadn't. She loved him. And his heart responded in kind.

Why, then, did he get the inescapable impression that it was over?

"Are you ready?" Anne-Marie asked.

Josie didn't appear to hear at first, then she slowly tugged her gaze away from Drew's and nodded. "Yes."

But Drew wasn't ready. Nowhere near ready. He wanted to haul her to him and hold her so tightly that she could never walk away from him.

He wasn't sure who was more surprised when he did just that, folding her into his arms, breathing in the smoky scent of her hair and skin, wishing for everything he was worth that the fear filling him was a figment of his imagination.

"Come back to Kansas City with me," he said, grasping her arms. "I'll take care of you."

She smiled in a way he hadn't seen her smile before. With sadness. With love.

"No, Drew…I can't."

She freed a hand from the blanket and cupped the side of his face, running her thumb along his jawline.

"This is home for me."

Drew felt like he'd been sucker punched. "Josie, the hotel is gone."

She didn't say anything for a moment, then she shook her head. "The Josephine will go on, Drew. Just as she always has."

She removed her hand, her eyes beseeching. "We both knew from the beginning that this would end. That you would go back to Kansas City. The circumstances may have changed, but that never has."

Had she just said it was over?

"I'm coming back," he said resolutely.

She smiled wearily and tucked her chin into her chest. "I love you, Drew. Remember that always."

And just like that, she turned and walked out of his life.

"JOSIE! MON DIEU, what's going on?"

It took a moment for Josie to register that someone had directed a question toward her. She'd just left Drew standing looking at her as if she'd removed his heart straight from his chest. And she felt like someone had done the same to her.

Saying goodbye to him had to be the most difficult thing she'd ever done in her life. Including watching the Josephine burn. Never would she have believed that to be possible. The hotel was her family, her legacy. And Drew…

Drew was the love of her life.

She found her hand moving as if on its own accord to her flat belly beneath the blanket, hope blossoming within her that she'd be blessed with a small reminder of him, of their sweet time together.

"Jesus, girl, are you okay?"

Josie blinked at the woman in front of her. She hadn't realized that she was there until then.

Her cousin.

To her surprise, Sabine hugged her almost as tightly as Drew had moments before.

"A friend ran to my place to tell me the news." She held Josie at arm's length. "Are you all right?"

Josie nodded, the genuine concern on her cousin's face was too much to bear in light of everything else happening.

Sabine's gaze went to the hotel and the firemen swarming around and through it.

"Is the hotel…I mean, will…"

Josie should have known there was an ulterior motive for her cousin's appearance. Oh, sure, she hadn't wanted to see Josie injured or harmed, but her ultimate goal was always the hotel and whatever money she could milk out of it.

Josie thought of the money in the lockbox she'd safely placed in the bag over her shoulder. Should she offer her cousin a cut? Pay her off and get her to release all claim?

Sabine pulled her to her side and they both stared at the Josephine.

"I'll help you put her to right."

Josie squinted at her.

"What? You think I'm only interested in the cash? The Josephine is…well, the Josephine. The Quarter wouldn't be the same without her here."

Josie wasn't sure which shocked her more: that Sabine was saying the words or that she apparently appeared to mean them.

"I mean, if you'll let me help you…"

Josie stared at her. It had been a year since *Granme* had passed. A year of troubles and hardships, including from the woman at her side. Did Josie dare invite more?

She smiled. "I'd love it if you'd help," she murmured. "After all, this is a family thang."

They laughed together and Josie felt some of the weight lift off her shoulders.

As they continued walking in the direction of Anne-Marie's place, the other two women chatting about what had happened, Josie looked over her shoulder at the Josephine, where the charred fourth floor was still emitting smoke.

For a startling moment, she could have sworn she saw her *granme* there, her arms crossed, smiling down at Josie. And instead of smelling smoke, she detected narcissus.

Then she looked at where Drew still stood, staring at her helplessly.

It took every ounce of effort she could drag up, but she managed to turn and continue walking, determined not to look back again.

21

DREW STOOD LOOKING OUT the window of his office in downtown Kansas City, the phone to his ear. He was on hold. Which pretty much reflected the state of the rest of his life: it was all on hold.

He dry-washed his face with his free hand then turned from the window, blind to his posh surroundings. He'd opened the office some six years ago, prior to that his home office having sufficed, especially given the traveling involved in his job.

Correction: the traveling his job had once entailed.

He sat at his desk, the antique leather chair giving a low squeak. It was impossible to believe that just over two weeks had passed since he'd left New Orleans. Half a month since he'd drunk in Josie's beautiful face. Sixteen days since he'd held her in his arms. He'd picked up the phone no fewer than a dozen times to call her, then replaced the receiver, determining that it was better if he not make contact. At least not yet. Not until he was done with what he needed to do.

Because when he returned to New Orleans this time, he meant to stay for good.

He looked around at the panoramic view of the midwestern city outside his window, at the signs of autumn, the heat of the Crescent City far away. His surroundings couldn't have been more different from those in which Josie had been raised. But the city had never really been home. It was familiar, yes. But his brief marriage to Carol aside, he'd never felt a burning need to return here. It had just been a place where he owned a home. There was nothing wrong with Kansas City. The place had been good to him. And it's where he was from.

But it wasn't where Josie was.

And wherever Josie was, that was home for him.

He hung up the phone and contacted his assistant. "Get my attorney back on the line, Janice. I was cut off," he lied.

Truth was he felt like every ticking second was an eternity. And that it put him farther and farther away from Josie.

The telephone rang and he snatched it up.

"Arnold, I need—"

"Drew?"

A female voice. His heart skipped a beat.

"This is Carol."

His ex-wife.

He rested his elbow against the desk and scratched his head. For a moment, a precious moment, he'd thought it was Josie. Instead, it was a woman who couldn't be more different from the woman he loved.

"What is it, Carol?" he tried to keep the impatience from his voice, but failed. He really didn't want to be speaking to her right now. She was part of his past. And he only had room for the future.

"I…" She hesitated.

He closed his eyes. He hadn't heard from her since she'd made off with his personal savings and the contents of his house. Even then, she'd gotten half the worth of the house in the final settlement.

Of course, he was a man who'd once lived for his career, which meant most of his capital had been tied up in his company, untouchable by Carol and her lawyer.

"I just called to see how you're doing."

He squinted at the framed diplomas on the opposite wall. "I'm sorry if I'm having a hard time believing that."

Silence, then she said, "Do you think you'll ever be able to forgive me, Drew?"

No. It was on the tip of his tongue. And would have launched right off it only three weeks ago.

Now, however, he held on to it, no matter how much it choked him. Although he really wasn't sure why.

"What do you want, Carol?"

She didn't say anything for a long moment and he made out the sound of a car horn in the background of wherever she was calling from. Her cell? Seemed likely.

"Drew, I'm in trouble."

He clenched his jaw, his suspicions confirmed. She needed money.

"It's not what you think," she said quickly. "I've been thinking about you a lot lately."

He bet she had. Trying to find a way to tap into even more of his cash.

"You got enough from me to set you up for life," he said.

If she worked it right, invested a good chunk of the funds, perhaps started up a business of her own.

"My attorney and his accountant made off with most of it. I have a hundred dollars to my name."

"And that affects me how?" he couldn't keep himself from saying.

"Drew, I…I know you have a lot of cause to be

angry with me. What I did to you…it was horrible. I know that now.…"

"An epiphany caused by your current circumstances."

"No! I mean, I'm calling you because of that, but I knew pretty much immediately that what I'd done was wrong."

Silence.

Drew thought maybe she'd given him up as a lost cause and had hung up.

But then she spoke. "We were married for years, Drew. I made a mistake. A stupid mistake that I justified because you loved your job more than you loved me."

He didn't say anything.

"Look, I'm not going to make any excuses. It was wrong, and I'm apologizing."

"In the hopes of…" he prompted.

"In the hopes that we can be friends."

Friends.

While every other part of the conversation was somewhat familiar to him, sounded like things Carol would say to get what she wanted, the friends part caught him off guard.

He wouldn't have put it past her to suggest reconciliation. Perhaps even say she still loved him in order to get what she wanted.

But she hadn't done either.

An image of Josie's face crowded his mind. He sat back in his chair and loosened his tie.

A buzz, then Janice's voice on the speaker said, "Mr. Morrison, I have your attorney on line two."

He didn't move for an extended moment.

It wasn't all that long ago that he would have told his ex where to get off. Fool me once, shame on you. Fool me twice, shame on me.

But he no longer lived by that motto. No longer subscribed to much of the BS he'd convinced himself of before. Josie had changed all that. Loving Josie had changed all that.

He also knew that if he didn't help Carol, no one would.

"How much do you need?" he asked.

She named a reasonable amount.

"I'll give you double," he said, looking around the office. "But I have a favor to ask in return…."

JOSIE DIDN'T HAVE TO TAKE the test, she already knew: she was pregnant with Drew's child.

She stood in the bathroom of 2C, where Drew had stayed just over two weeks ago, and the room she'd called home for the past week. The insurance company had been cooperative. The first piece of business had been to stabilize the fourth floor so that the rest of the hotel would be operable while the top floor was being rebuilt.

She shook the testing stick although the directions had told her not to, stepping into the other room and looking around at the little she'd been able to salvage from the burned husk of what had been her and *Granme*'s private rooms. Some photos, her grandmother's rocking chair, a trunk of her older clothes. Everything else she'd needed had been supplied by Sabine and Anne-Marie—who'd, strangely, become fast friends, so close, in fact, that Josie was beginning to experience pangs of jealousy. The two women had taken her shopping, displaying a generosity that had humbled her.

While the room no longer looked like the one Drew had stayed in, and also didn't resemble her old room, she was okay with that. It reflected where she was now. And that was a very good place, indeed.

The Josephine would survive. Better, guests were already returning, the occupancy level at half and another guest looking to check in when Josie had sneaked up to her room during her dinner break to perform the test.

The test!

She'd almost forgotten about the stick. She

stopped shaking it. A green dot had appeared in the once-white area.

She smiled, her hand already resting against her still flat stomach.

"Josie, tell Anne-Marie that I'm entitled to see everything that comes into—"

Sabine and Anne-Marie had let themselves into the room and caught sight of what Josie was holding before she could hide it behind her back.

"What is this?" Anne-Marie asked, plucking the test stick from behind her.

Sabine stepped up next to her. "A pregnancy test?"

Anne-Marie stared at her. "What does it say?"

She didn't think she was ready to share this information yet. She wanted to savor the moment a little longer before letting her cousin and friend in on it.

Still, the news was too good to keep. "I'm pregnant."

She wasn't sure what the response would be. She was a single woman with a hotel under renovation and enough work ahead of her to keep ten women busy. How could she bring a child into that environment?

The same way her mother and her grandmother and her great grandmother before her had.

The Villefranche women's tradition continued.

Sabine was the first to whoop with joy as she hugged first Josie, then Anne-Marie, to her surprise.

"A girl! I know it's a girl. The Villefranche women don't know how to have anything but girls."

"You can't know that," Anne-Marie objected, hugging Josie and looking at her closely. She smiled. "Josie here might just be the first to break the tradition."

Josie took the stick from her friend and slid it into her dress pocket. "What did you two want to talk to me about?" she asked.

Anne-Marie held up an envelope. "I caught Sabine about to open this."

Her cousin spoke up. "I was tidying the front desk and happened to come across it, that's all. She doesn't have to make a capital crime out of it."

Josie's chest tightened as she took the familiar envelope. It had been locked in the cash box, so Sabine hadn't been merely cleaning up, she'd been snooping.

The envelope held Drew's name.

"Hey, isn't he the guy you were with when the fire started?" Sabine asked.

"Shush, girl," Anne-Marie told her. "You have all the manners of a goat."

Josie didn't have to open the envelope to know

what was inside. She'd read the note no fewer than a hundred times since she'd received it two days after she and Drew had said goodbye.

But she hadn't done anything about the hefty check that had come with it.

"Something to tide you over until we meet again," the note read. "Love, Drew."

"It's a check," Sabine told Anne-Marie. "But I didn't see for how much."

Josie tucked the envelope into her pocket along with the test stick. "It doesn't matter. I'm not going to cash it."

"Why not?" both women asked in unison.

Josie stared at them, then led the way out of the room and down the stairs to the front desk where Monique was quickly stubbing out a ciga-rette. She instantly got up and, murmuring some-thing under her breath about having to come and clean rooms on her off hours, disappeared back into the kitchen, her maid's uniform rustling.

"Look," Anne-Marie said, slapping her hand on the desk when Josie rounded it. "You have more than yourself to think about now. View it as a sort of child support…in advance."

Sabine agreed. "It's a damn sight more than any of the Villefranche women got from the fathers of their children."

"That's because the fathers never knew of the children's existence."

"Same difference."

"No, it's not," Josie said, the switch in conversation feeding directly into the dilemma she faced.

In the previous Villefranche women's cases, it had been different times, and they hadn't known how to contact the men who had fathered their children. Josie had an address for Drew right in her pocket.

Should she tell him? Did he want to know?

"If you don't want the check, I'll take it," Sabine said.

Josie frowned at her. Her cousin was still on the public dole. Granted, she'd only worked at the hotel for a week so that could change. And at some point when the hotel was doing better, Josie hoped to put Sabine on the deed, which might make her feel more confident financially. But Josie was determined to get her cousin to listen to the voices of the women who had come before them. To get her to stand on her own feet and make do for herself rather than believing she was owed.

But there would be time for that.

She smiled as she smoothed her hand over her stomach. There would be time for everything.

The sun was beginning to set on the street outside and no one had turned on the lobby lights yet aside from the desk lamp. She wasn't sure what compelled her to look in the direction of the door. A ghostly hand on her shoulder. A familiar scent.

Whatever the reason, she stood stock-still at the image she encountered.

A man in a neat, navy-blue business suit stood there, hat in his hand, an expensive brown leather suitcase on the banquette next to his feet.

Drew.

Anne-Marie and Sabine were chatting. It was her friend who first caught on to Josie's distracted state. She looked in the direction of Josie's gaze.

"Uh-huh. Speak of the devil."

Devil? No, Drew was no devil. He was her savior. A man who had entered her life, and lied to her, then given her his love, and shown her what the word was all about.

And just as he'd promised, he had come back.

22

THERE SHE STOOD BEHIND the freshly varnished front desk of the Josephine. A burst of color in Drew's gray world. The last two torturous weeks between the time she'd left him standing on the street and this moment disappeared as if they had never existed.

Josie…

The two women she stood with—he absently recognized one as Anne-Marie—became aware of his presence and disappeared back into the kitchen.

That left him and Josie alone, staring at each other.

Drew picked up his suitcase and stepped inside the lobby, much as he had on that fateful day just over three weeks ago. Had it really only been that long? How quickly Josie had become an important part of his life, of his heart. So much so that he couldn't remember what life had been like without her.

What he had been like without her.

Drew couldn't begin to reconcile the old him with the one who wanted to be a better man for Josie. His entire philosophy had changed as a result of her love. And while he felt a healthy portion of trepidation about the shift in his life's direction, he also knew that it was for the better. And no matter what happened in these next few moments, the changes were permanent.

Whatever transpired, he was glad to be here now, rather than at an unspecified time down the road. In a roundabout way, Carol had done him a bigger favor than he'd done her. By agreeing to close up his office and handle any on-site details in Kansas City, she had freed him up to return home.

He put his suitcase down before the front desk. "Do you have any rooms available?" he asked with a hesitant smile.

Josie's heart was beating so loudly she nearly didn't hear Drew's quietly spoken question.

Truthfully, she hadn't expected to see him again. She'd been convinced that what they'd had, what they'd shared, would be forever relegated to a special corner of the past. Never once had she allowed herself to indulge in the fantasy of his returning. To New Orleans. To her.

She removed her hand from where it lay against her belly as if protecting the precious life growing within her. But protecting it from what, she couldn't be sure. From pain? From future hurt when Drew left again?

He placed a flyer that Sabine had distributed at the airport on the desk, much like the flyer he'd used the first time around. Josie didn't have to read it. The pink paper was enough to identify it.

"How long will you be needing the room?" she asked, her throat so tight she nearly couldn't speak as she turned toward the keys.

"Indefinitely."

She swiveled to stare at him.

He smiled, seeming more unsure of himself than she'd ever seen him. "Or at least until I can make, um, other arrangements."

"Other arrangements?"

A man she recognized as a taxi driver lugged in a couple of additional suitcases.

"Just put them over there," Drew said, indicating a spot near the bottom of the stairs.

The driver mopped his brow with a handkerchief, then tucked the white material back into his pocket. "I'll go get the rest."

The rest? Drew had *more* luggage?

Josie felt as if the floor had just shifted under her feet as the driver left them alone again.

"You didn't cash the check," Drew said quietly.

She was so stunned, there was a time delay between when words were said and when they actually registered in her mind.

"Are you really that surprised to see me?"

She nodded, feeling ridiculously close to tears.

Before she could blink them back, he rounded the desk and folded her into his arms. His wonderfully strong arms. A place she'd never thought she'd find herself again.

A place she never wanted to leave.

He smelled of fresh starch and a woodsy aftershave and Drew.

"Jesus," he murmured, seeming mesmerized as he looked over her face and into her eyes. "You really have no clue how I feel about you."

She shook her head. No, she knew. But she'd come to learn that feelings and actions were often two different things.

Until now...

He seemed to have forgotten something. While holding her close with one hand, he fished around inside his jacket.

"I would have been here sooner—hell, I would never have left at all—except I had some things to clean up first. Doors to close. Windows to open." He pulled out a packet of papers in a leather holder and handed them to her. "I know it's not an engagement ring, but I figured this would mean more to you. Jewelry we can go shopping for together tomorrow."

Jewelry?

Josie tried to make sense out of what he was saying.

"Take them," he urged.

"If it's another check…"

He smiled, skimming his thumb over her cheek then leaning in to kiss her.

Josie melted into him and her mind stopped working at all. Coherent thought gave over to pure instinct.

Oh, how she loved this man.

After long moments, he drew back. "Mmm." His eyes were dark, his breathing ragged. "We're going to have to stop doing that in public." He tugged at his collar. "Go on, read them."

Josie didn't think she'd be able to make out a single word, but she opened the envelope anyway and took out the papers. She made out one word at the top of the first page of many: *Deed*.

She blinked at him.

"Essentially that says you are now owner of the land surrounding the Josephine. Free and clear."

"What?"

He nodded. "That door I needed to close? It was

with my former client, who also employed Philippe."

She stared at him.

"No, I didn't know. I suspected there was someone else working the case, but I had no idea who. Needless to say, my client found himself between a rock and a hard place when Philippe was arrested for murder. News like that has been known to bring down the biggest of men."

She held the papers out to him. "I don't want these."

He chuckled softly. "Doesn't matter, Josie. They're yours to do with what you want." He looked around the lobby. "I thought you might want to expand the Josephine."

She remained silent for a minute, remembering all she'd gone through, all she continued to go through and what the Josephine represented for her. "No. The people who owned these businesses were probably forced into selling, much the same way they wanted to get me to sell."

He scanned her face. "Then give it back to them."

Josie's heart soared so high, she was afraid she'd never be able to cram it back into her chest.

His voice lowered. "Whatever you do, it's completely your decision."

The driver appeared in the doorway again, hauling additional bags even larger than the ones before. He was huffing and puffing and didn't look too happy.

"I'll…just…go…get…the last…bag," he said.

Josie couldn't help giggling.

Giggling! She couldn't remember when—if—she'd ever indulged in the carefree act, no matter how young, no matter how long ago.

"I hope you tipped him well."

"I did."

And she knew he had.

While Drew's actions in the beginning had been highly questionable, she knew in her bones that the man standing before her was a man of integrity, strength, goodness and love.

And she didn't know how she'd survived her life so far without him in it.

He slid his hand into his pants pocket. "I may not have been able to decide on a proper engagement ring, but…well…I hope you'll accept this until we can get you one you like."

Josie blinked at the band of tiny white shells that matched her anklet. They were so perfect, so small and so *her* that the tears that had threatened before stated rolling over her lashes.

"Uh-oh," he murmured, swiping the dampness from her right cheek with his thumb. "I'm not very savvy on the meaning of women's tears. You'll have to tell me—are these good or bad?"

She nodded, then shook her head. "It's…they are…I mean…oh, I don't know what I mean." She swallowed hard. "It's good."

"May I?"

She held up her trembling left hand so that he could slip the shell ring onto her finger.

"Will you marry me, Josie?" he whispered, seeming to look beyond the years of independence, of trying times, of lonely nights, into the very depths of her soul.

"Yes," she breathed.

There were hoots and hollers from around the corner. But Josie couldn't acknowledge them. All she could do was marvel at the difference one man could make.

Granme's words snaked through her mind as Drew held her so tightly she couldn't breathe. "*Sha bébé,* you must always listen to the little voice inside your head. While your heart may lead you astray, your head never will."

In that one moment, her heart and head were in complete agreement.

And just like that, the curse that had shadowed the Villefranche women for over two centuries was broken.

She smiled as she kissed Drew again and again. She couldn't wait to share her own little surprise with him. And for some reason she couldn't explain, she was convinced the life growing within her, the life they had created, would be a little boy.

With these women, being single never means being alone

Lauren, a divorced empty nester, has tricked her editor into thinking she is a twentysomething girl living the single life. As research for her successful column, she hits the bars, bistros, concerts and lingerie shops with her close friends. When her job requires her to make a live television appearance, can she keep her true identity a secret?

The Single Life
by Liz Wood